T0209183

RAPTURED GRACE

SHAKEN BUT NOT BROKEN

BOOK 5

A NOVEL

DR. AKEAM AMONIPHIS SIMMONS

RAPTURED GRACE
SHAKEN BUT NOT BROKEN

iUniverse books may be ordered through booksellers or by contacting:

iUniverse
1663 Liberty Drive
Bloomington, IN 47403
www.iuniverse.com
844-349-9409

ISBN: 978-1-6632-6033-8 (sc)
ISBN: 978-1-6632-6032-1 (e)

Library of Congress Control Number: 2024902894

Print information available on the last page.

iUniverse rev. date: 02/07/2024

To the thousands upon thousands of readers that shall read this book and the **Grace** novel series; may you walk in God's tender mercies and blessings! I love all of you!

CHAPTER ONE

Welcome Pandemonium

The Raptured

1 Thessalonians 4: 14-17

14. For if we believe that Jesus died and rose again, even so, them also which sleep in Jesus will God bring with him.

15. For this we say unto you by the word of the Lord, that we which are alive and remain unto the coming of the Lord shall not prevent them which are asleep.

16. For the Lord himself shall descend from heaven with a shout, with the voice of the archangel, and with the trump of God; and the dead in Christ shall rise first:

17. Then we which are alive and remain shall be caught u[together with them in the clouds, to meet the Lord in the air and s shall we ever be with the Lord.

Revelation 4: 1-2

1. After this I looked, and behold, a door was opened in heaven: and the first voice which I heard was as it ere of a trumpet talking with me; which said, Come up here, and I will show you things which must be hereafter.

2. And immediately I was in the spirit and behold a throne was set in heaven, and one sat on the throne.

The sky whistled and turned like a loud trumpet had sounded in the midst of a whirling wind, and then it violently sucked up itself like God was taking a deep labored breath, angry and repenting of the very creation that He had made.

Solemn grey clouds raced across the empty sky and rested just beyond the Sentinel Mountains off in the distance.

A violent wrathful wind blew hard from the East-like all the air was sucked up from the East and blown down on the inhabitants of the West; the sky churned and the earth rocked as a drunken man like it would never stop.

Airplanes began falling out of the sky and violently crashing to the ground as if on a single command-littering the ground with scattered fires and littered bodies everywhere-many severed and burned beyond recognition.

Trains derailed their tracks, while others just crashed violently into their waiting train stations; cars veered off the road and slammed into buildings, while others just crashed into the other cars on the roadway and many burst into flames.

It was as though Lady Calamity was angry at the people of earth and decided to extract her violent vengeances upon them-she had gripped the earth and wasn't soon to let go.

Anguish bitter tears flowed, like rivers from Zion, down streets riddle with anguish hurt and pain, for everybody had lost somebody. Someone was missing out of every home, and every family. Bitter tears perused every neighborhood on every street. Mothers were screaming for their missing children, husbands and wives were laboring for their missing spouses. It was happening all at the same time all over the world.

The whole earth had become a raging war zone; hopelessness spread like a disease; everywhere someone was wailing.

V walked briskly back down the trouble infested streets from whence she had just accompanied Willie. Her mind raced, filled with the bombardment of a thousand hyperventilating questions; of which she had no answer to, and her subconscious woman told her that she really didn't want to fully know.

She wanted to stop and rest; she needed to stop and rest, but the upheaval stirring in her bosom wouldn't allow her to. She had to press on; had to find her love, Snow, the one that made her whole; the one that completed her. She just couldn't live without him, and she didn't want to; so she pressed onward, ignoring the pain throbbing in her feet and her aching back shooting fiery pain up to the base of her neck.

Angry lowering red pinkish clouds raced across the billowing grey sky, like a lioness about to pounce upon a helpless unsuspecting fawn. Every now- and- then, thunder rumbled and shouted loudly as mesmerizing flashes of blinding lightening streaked wildly across the never ending heavens. The winds shifted and hissed down the wailing streets filled with unbeknown, unsuspecting victims of mayhem; blowing some people clean off their feet and tossing them violently down the streets. Women screamed; men bellowed hard from a place deep within them that no man wants to succumb to or even admit exist deep down in the crevasses of his very soul; all feeling helpless caught fighting mother nature while she spew out her scorn upon those that had taken her for granted and destroyed much of her forestry from the beginning of time, to satisfy their never ending greed.

People were weeping, hollering, and crying everywhere. The streets were filled with lamenting men and women, but no children to be seen or found anywhere. It seemed that all innocence had vanished while the wicked, unprepared, and irreverent filled and roamed the torned rock and reeling streets in disbelief of the mayhem.

Buildings were on fire with no fire trucks to be seen or heard. Carnage engulfed the whole city and probably the whole world, or at least it felt that way to the tormented victims perusing the tormented streets.

Masses of people and all children had simply vanished in a whiff of a moment without any hint or warning. Women frantically searched for their children as tears drenched their cheeks and nestled under their chin.

No land lines, cell phones, or internet anywhere-all were blacked out with no signal to be even heard; no electricity, and gas lines were broken; the smell of gas infiltrated the air with explosions engulfing buildings and gas stations from one street to another. Houses were engulfed in flames and just burned to the ground. Everyone screamed and yelled for help, but there was none to be given-even fire stations burned to the ground.

V wondered, as she cautiously looked around, has the whole world gone crazy. Nothing made sense. The tears refused to stop running down her cheeks.

Suddenly, an old wrecked gun and ammunition shop caught her eye. She knew that she only had a few rounds left in her 9; so she raced over to the dilapidated building, barely still standing with windows burst out and a buzzing alarm that had grown tired of screaming.

Swiftly she crossed the street and hesitantly entered the gun store. There were weapons everywhere; some lying in broken display cases; just lying there for whoever would take them.

Quickly she grabbed up two 9s, and then looked around for clips and bullets. She found them in several crushed drawers. V loaded five clips and filled her half empty clip that she already had. When she was about to leave, she noticed a shotgun hanging on the wall. She grabbed it and found the shells, loaded the shotgun and slung it across her shoulder. She saw a backpack, grabbed it and filled it full of buck shots and more bullets for her 9s. V was ready for whatever she might face-she would shoot them to hell and back, she thought anxiously to herself.

She then rushed out, heart racing, breathing heavily, and back across the street. She peeped across her shoulder as she exited the gun store.

The streets were yet filled with screaming, and people weeping and moaning everywhere. She kept pushing forward, ignoring everybody, with only the thought of Snow, her beloved, forever burned into her mind.

V kept going; she couldn't stop, wouldn't stop. People were everywhere. She saw a bunch of thugs standing on the corner looking for an opportunity. She put her hand on her 9 and eased it from her side. She wouldn't hesitate to pop one of them, or even all of them if she had to; for she refused to be their opportunity.

In the back of her mind, she hoped that they would do something. She needed some relief, and this was just the fix she needed- to pop even one of them would relieve some of the stress built up in her chest and rested on her shoulders.

"Hey little cutie." One of them asked (even though her gun was plain to see), giggling as he did. "What you got in that bag? You got more guns or something?"

"She ain't gone shoot nobody," another one shouted out as they surrounded her. "She ain't got the guts."

"Just try me?" V growled, staring hard at them. "Just try me? Please try me. See don't I send you to hell quicker than you can blink your creepy little eyes."

"Just give us your stuff and we'll let you get on your way." Another of them hissed at her.

"Nooo, we gone have a lil fun with you before you go." A short straggly one said. "Don't you want to have a lil party with us before you go on your way?"

They started to move in closer to V, getting ready to jump on her and take whatever they wanted, including her.

Pow! Pow! Her gun shouted into the air. V shot two of them without even flinching, and then turned the 9 at another one of them.

"Ok, who's next? Is that enough fun for you-huh? Is it?" V hissed like an angry lioness protecting her cubs. "Who else is ready to die? I'll send all of yawl to hell today-just try me…. Please try me!"

"She just shot me Bro; she just shot me!" One of the wounded men sang out as he lay on the hard pavement waddling in pain and rich red blood. "She shot me! Why you shoot me? We were just having fun. You shot me! Cray woman shot me."

"You bet I did." V exclaimed loudly, getting ready to send another hot bullet racing their way. "Who's next? I'll send all of you to hell today. Just try me! Just try me!" She screamed loudly at the now fleeing men-leaving their wounded comrades behind in a blaze of fear and pain.

"We'll see you later miss gunslinger." One of them yelled back at her, obviously in fear, trying to dispel his embarrassment of being ran off by a woman.

"Not if I see you first." She said evenly, still pointing the 9 at them with her finger resting on the trigger. "Cock roaches!"

They all scattered and ran off into the distance, leaving one of their friends lying on the ground holding his stomach in pain while another lay a foot from him silent and unconscious.

"Should have killed all of them cock roaches." She moaned angrily to herself. "Saved the next person they going to attack like dogs. Dog gone cockroaches!"

She had been walking now for about an hour when she eased upon and old candy apple red 1968 Ford Mustang fastback GT500 with 460 Horse power. It looked fast, and it was screaming her name.

V slowed her cadence and slowly looked the car over; then she looked around to see if anyone was watching her; and although the streets were filled with wailing people, morning, hurting people, everybody was minding their own business, or lack thereof anyway.

She slid her hand slowly down the side of the slick car, imagining the wind blowing through her hair as she sliced the air, racing down the streets.

V looked around again, still no one seemed to be paying her any attention.

"It belonged to Joe; my husband who disappeared with the rest of the folks." An old silver haired lady, in a dark drab dress and dirty grease spotted spattered apron wedged around her waist, said as she exited the darkened building where the car was parked in front of. "You like it?"

"Yes mam. I love it." V said, allowing her mind to ease and wonder for a moment. She slowly slid the palm of her hand down the side of the car.

"What's your name?" The old lady asked heartedly, but smooth.

"Veronica, but everybody calls me V."

"Please to meet you V. Names Mary; everybody calls me Big Mary except the children; they calls me Miss Mary."

"I'll sale it to ya for one of them guns you got on your side." Big Mary continued.

"Huh?" The old lady's offer startled V. She rested her hand on the handle of her 9, not fully knowing what to expect from the old lady. "You want to sell it? Why? For what?"

"For one of them guns; I need some protection now that my man is gone." The old lady said, now resting her hands on her full round hips.

"You would?" V managed to say. "Like a sheep amongst a pack of wolves-you right, sooner or later, they gone try to eat you."

"Yea. I know. I ain't got no use for it, and it ain't long before them young thugs come to my store to take something from me." She said. "And I want to greet them properly so they won't want to come back to grandma's store no more."

"You sure?" V stumbled to say, not believing what she was hearing. She had anticipated, at least a hard bargain with the old lady.

"Yea, is it a deal?" Big Mary said, shuffling over to the other side of the front of her store. "Sure as I ever been about anything."

"Do you know how to shoot?" V questioned the old lady, not sure whether to take her serious or not.

"There be a lot of thangs grandma can't do, but shooting a gun ain't one of them. Husband taught me that a long time ago." She said, stepping a little closer to V. "Guess he knew something like this was going to happen. Lord knows I didn't go to church like I was supposed to. I thought that I had plenty of time like the rest of them fools wondering around here; no offense baby."

"None taken," said V stepping back, not fully trusting the old lady.

"You don't have to worry about me sweetie." She said. "Big Mary ain't never hurt nobody that didn't deserve it. You look like a sweetheart just in a bad time. Grandma understands."

"Ok." V said, still cautious.

"So, is it a deal, or are you gone let them thugs take all I got and kill me too?"

"Does it run." V asked.

"Does it run-huh? Roars like a lion and runs like a cheetah." She said. "You get in that baby ain't nobody gone catch you except the ones you want to."

"Ok, where is the key?"

"Over the visor on the driver's side." Big Mary pointed at the visor as she spoke with a long grin of satisfaction on her face.

V leaned into the window, let down the visor and grabbed the key. She stood back up, tossed the key up and down in her palm and thought to herself, "Yes, this is a game changer." She whispered softly to herself.

She reached in her back pack, grabbed one of the 9s, two clips, and handed it to the old lady.

"Yea, this gone make a difference; yes-sir- ree." The old lady said softly.

"I need you to write me some kind of Bill of sale." She said. "Just in case the cops stop me."

"What cops? Child they got their hands full if there is any left; cause what I hear on the radio is that everybody is missing somebody, and child they say that it has happened all over the world." She whipped back at V as a solemn look eased upon her burrow riddled face. "Cops too busy looking for their own to worry bout us. No, we've got to take care of ourselves right now sugar."

"Well." V started to say.

"I'll write something down on a piece of paper for you if that will make you happy. You ain't gone need it though."

The old lady turned and went back into the store as she pushed the clip into her newly acquired 9.

The sound of the clip made V nervous, so she, again, rested her hand on the handle of her ready 9.

"Great!" She moaned to herself.

After a few minutes had passed, she came back out with a piece of paper, and handed it to V.

"Thank you; take care of yourself, and I'll be praying for you." V said uneasily, but she thought that it would make the old lady feel better.

"Yea, me too, cause God is the only one that can get us through these times." The old lady mumbled as she disappeared back into the darkened store.

"Hey Miss Mary….Miss Mary." V yelled after her.

The old lady came back to the door and veered hard at V, now wondering what could she possibly need now.

"What is it child? What do you want now, but it's alright because I like your company- Gets awfully lonely round here sometimes."

"You got any water you can spare?" V asked softly.

"Don't have that much, but I guess I can give you a few bottles. The water from the faucets is now so bitter; don't know what's wrong with it, but I guess I ought to be thankful because it was red as blood last week. I don't know what's going on; it smelled like blood-real blood. How can blood come from the faucet? Somebody must have died in the water system; now it's bitter and smells like wormwood- probably poisoned."

"I know; the hold water system is probably bad because of all of this stuff that is going on." V replied.

She went back into the store, and in a few minutes later, came back with several bottles of water; then handed them to V.

"Sip on them wisely cause that's hard to come by now a days –fresh clean water."

V got into the mustang, started it up, and just like the old lady had said, it roared when she pressed on the gas. She pushed down the clutch and put it in first gear.

"Hey, hey, V…..V!" A voice screamed out from across the street. "V, hold up. Hold up."

It was Willie running towards her, almost out of breath.

She peered through her rearview mirror. Who could possibly be calling her name? She knew no one on this side of town, and then she recognized Willie.

"Where you going?" He asked, leaning on the car, struggling to catch his breath.

"What in the world; I thought that you were back with your family." V said to Willie with raised eye brows of pleasant surprise.

"No, they gone too." Willie said softly, lowing his head sadly in the locks of his shoulders. "Quitta and my daughter are both gone. I guess I ought to be thankful, seeing that I know where they went. Just hate that I missed it. All that preaching in vain; no, not in vain, I guess I just wasn't listening to my own sermons."

"Sorry to hear that Willie." V moaned softly. "Everybody done lost somebody; a lot of tears being shed now-a-days."

"Well, they are in a better place; much better than where we are." He said, trying to assure himself. "Where you going?"

"I am going to find Snow, and I don't know if that is even possible, but I got to try." She said, looking off in the distance, remembering a few past gone memories.

"Huh?" Willie's eyes bucked; looking at V in disbelief. "You sure you want to do that?"

"Yea, I am going back to my man come hell or high water; I am going back." She said looking firmly back at Willie. "What are you going to do now?"

"I am going where you are going-back to the church with you where we last saw Snow; though I doubt if anybody is there. Shoot, Snow probably done killed them all." He realized what he had said when V shot a piercing evil look at him. "My bag. Um sorry; I wasn't thinking."

"You usually aren't." V snapped at him, looking straight ahead. Well, you'd better get in and fasten your seatbelt."

Willie leaped into the car, fastened his seatbelt, and looked over at V questioningly.

"What?" She asked.

"Nothing."

"What Willie?" V snapped.

"Ah, you sure you want to go back where Snow is. You do remember what we saw when we last left him, or have you forgotten?"

"Yea, I remember, but its Snow, and I can't just give up on him now when he needs me the most. God knows he has saved my butt more times than I can count." She said, staring straight ahead. "And yes, um a little scared and a lil nervous, but I got to go. I have no choice."

"The red devilish eyes, and the 666 in his palm; you remember that don't you?" Willie questioned.

"Yea Willie, I remember." She snapped, now irritated with him. She desperately tried to deny what she had seen on her beloved Snow, but her memory refused to die.

"Signs of the antichrist; that's what the bible says anyway." Willie mumbled to himself.

"Um still going anyway Willie. Now, are you in or out cause Um about to leave." V snapped angrily at him; although secretly, she knew that Willie was telling the truth.

"Ok, Ok, I guess it's good to know the antichrist personally-huh." He replied under his breath sarcastically."

He looked down on the floor of the car and saw the three bottles of water. "Can I have one? Been a minute since I had a drink of water."

"Yea, but drink it wisely because I am told that all the water is either blood or bitter like wormwood."

"Yea, don't surprise me because that's what the bible says is part of the judgment." Willie said while grabbing the bottle of water, popping the cap, and chugging down a large mouth full.

V just rolled her eyes over at him, popped the clutch and pressed the gas pedal to the floor. The engine roared; the tires hollered and squealed, leaving smoke and black tire marks on the road.

Willie was pinned to his seat while the mustang zoomed past other cars, some overturned. Wailing people littered the streets trying to find hope amidst all of the ever consuming hopelessness.

She popped second gear, and again the back tires hollered out, and reached for more road.

"Yes, this baby is the truth." V bellowed in excitement. "Aaahhhh yesssss! She screamed into the air in excitement mingled with fear.

"What in the world. You trying to kill us?" Willie hollered out, digging his fingers into the side of the seat. "I want to go to heaven but not today."

"Just hold on man; hold on." V said, shifting into third gear.

Willie sat there terrified; not knowing whether he was going to live or die in the hands of this crazy love driven woman driving a muscle car that wasn't taking any prisoners. He thought of jumping out but the thought of slamming into the hard pavement quickly dissipated that thought.

"Ohhhhh Jesus help us!" Willie screamed out, still digging his fingers into the side of the seat with his eyes now tightly shut.

"That's right! That's right! The best thing you can do is pray, or shut up and try to enjoy this hell of a ride-even if it does take us straight to hell. Yesssssss!" V screamed out while popping the last gear.

The golden sun eased slowly back over the trees, standing silently reaching up to the heavens like sentinels waiting on their command. The red billowing clouds rolled back from whence they had come to give way to the glimmering stars that silently glistened in the never ending sky. Crickets began to sing the chorus of their nightly melody, chiming that night was on the way, while other nocturnal creatures dawn the creaks and crevasses of the turmoil stricken streets of fore longing and uncertainty.

The candy apple red mustang zoomed down the streets like a bat out of hell bent on destruction.

V didn't know what she would find, or even who Snow was now, but she knew that staying put was not an option. She had to go to her beloved-no matter the consequences.

Willie just sat there, eyes still shut, and silently prayed-hoping that this was a dream, or at least for a better tomorrow. He hoped upon hope that he had not put his life in the hands of a crazy woman driven and blinded by love.

CHAPTER TWO

LEFT BEHIND

Revelations 6: 7-8

7. And when he had opened the fourth seal, I heard a voice of the fourth beast say come and see.

8. And I looked, and behold, a pale horse; and his name that sat on him was death, and hell followed with him. And power was given them over the fourth part of the earth, to kill with sword, and with hunger, and with death, and with the beasts of the field

Nestled deeply, in the heart of the unforgiving neighborhood, amongst shotgun houses and falling down government projects apartments, Pa Frank, Mr. Pocket, and Archie sat outside Pa Frank's old dilapidated corner store watching all the chaos engulfing them and their neighbors. Grief catapulted upon them and rested on their shoulders like hungry vultures waiting for their prey to die.

Streams of black smoke from buildings all over the city eased up to the angry sky and licked lazy waterless clouds. Buildings simmered and burned everywhere; not enough fire stations to control all the fires that ravaged the city as it pleased. They just burned themselves out. And, many that was not burning or smoking were crumbled with people still inside of them while their love ones wailed and searched; hoping upon hope that all was not lost.

Wild animals had left their natural habitat and roamed the tormented streets searching for an opportune meal- oftentimes, it was a helpless family or a lone wayward man that was searching for someone-a wife, children, or friends, just anyone to help make sense of what they were going through. Many of them watched in horror as they witness someone being devoured by a pack of dogs; and snakes were everywhere, as though the sky itself had decided to rain down snakes. Just down the street a hungry anaconda was swallowing a man as some scared terrified peopled tried vainly to help the already dead man.

All civilization as we know it was gone and plummeted back into a time long forgotten.

Screaming sirens and blasting alarms shouted in the air, beckoning for anyone's help. Every face was showered with tears and fears.

Overturned cars and trucks crowded the streets with fallen planes and overturned trains littering adjacent fields-some half buried beneath the ground with luggage and bodies strolled everywhere.

Civilization as they knew it was now gone-thrusted back to a time long ago forgotten, where only the strong survived while they plagued the weak.

No phone, no electricity, and no running water-all were hopeless, just hopeless.

"What are we going to do yawl?" Pa Frank said glaring over, worriedly, at Mr. Pocket and Archie. "What are we gone do?"

"What can we do? It's just hopeless." Mr. Pocket eased out softly while taking in as much of the calamity as he could. "God help us."

"Yea, that's an understatement," whipped Archie.

"Hold on." Pa Frank said as he walked briskly back into his store.

"Where you going?" Mr. Archie said glaring over at him.

"I'll be right back." Pa Frank said evenly. "Just hold on a minute. Something we should have been doing all along."

After a few minutes had passed, Pa Frank burst through the doors with an old bible in his hands.

"What's that for?" Mr. Pocket asked, shifting in his stance and glaring down at the black book. "Too late for that Bro. You should have been reading that a long time ago. If you had, we wouldn't be in this mess that we're in. God help us!"

"Ain't never too late to start, as long as breath is in your body." Pa Frank snapped at Pocket; still looking down and perusing through the pages of the bible.

"What you looking for?" Pa Frank said, rubbing his age worn hands nervously through his peppered grey hair. "On the other hand, maybe I don't want to know; knowing you."

"What's coming next, and how do we handle it. It's all right here in the book of Revelations. I heard my mama talk of it many many times before. It's about to be some hell on earth. Now is a good time for us to accept The Lord Jesus as our savior."

"We already did; didn't we?" Mr. Pocket said, not really sure of what he was saying. "We joined the church didn't we? And, we attend sometimes, though, I must say, not as often as we should>"

"No, we didn't accept Him; we just joined a church, and visited there sometimes." Pa Frank said as he flipped through the pages-looking for everything and anything that would console them right now.

"Well, what does the bible say is next to happen?" Mr. Archie whipped, looking at them with wide eyes.

"All the Believers have been taken up to heaven; now let's see what happens next." Pa Frank mustered, flipping through the pages of the old timed riddled bible. "Now, um about to read parts of the ninth chapter of the book of Revelation-from verse thirteen to nineteen. Listen."

Pa Frank read slowly and evenly, "13. And the sixth angel sounded, and I heard a voice from the four horns of the golden altar which is before

God; 14. Saying to the sixth angel which had the trumpet, Loose the four angels which are bound in the great river Euphrates. 15. And the four angels were loosed, which were prepared for an hour, and a day, and a month, and a year, for to slay the third part of men. 16. And the number of the army of the horsemen were two hundred thousand thousand: and I heard the number of them. 17. And thus I saw the horses in the vision, and them that sat on them, having breastplates of fire, and of jacinth, and brimstone: and the heads of the horses were as the heads of lions; and out of their mouths issued fire and smoke and brimstone. 18. By these three was the third part of men killed, by the fire, and by the smoke, and by the brimstone, which issued out of their mouths. 19. For their power is in their mouth, and in their tails: for their tails were like unto serpents, and had heads, and with them they do hurt."

Archie and Mr. Pocket just stood there staring at Pa Frank in bewilderment with their mouths hanging open like they had seen a ghost.

"Lord help us," said Pa Frank.

"What are we gone do?" Mr. Pocket said, rubbing his hand through his grey shaggy beard. "Or better still, how we gone kill them damned things?"

"If I see something like that, um a tell you what um going to do." Archie whipped, waiting for them to ask him what was he going to do.

"Ok...Ok...What?" Pa Frank said, leaning into him. "What you gone do? What can you do?"

"Um a run like I never ran before; that's what um a do. That thing is gone have to catch my black butt running." Mr Pocket said before Archie could answer.

They all burst into laughter.

"You know you crazy don't you," said Pa Frank.

"Yea, but it's always better to say there he goes, than there he lays."

"I mean, did you guys hear what I just read? It's coming, or is already here; and that's not the worst of it. There is much more coming after those creatures, but before then, some other things have to happen."

"Like what? I mean, what can be worse than a horse with the head of a fire breathing lion and a tail of a snake; and it is 200,000.000 of them. That is more than all the people on the earth-several times over; and, you say that it's going to get worse-huh, I don't see how." Mr. Pocket exclaimed, now clearly shaken. "We need to pray, ah, what they call it-the sinner's prayer."

"Yea, um with you right there bro." Archie shouted, waving his hands in the air. "Let's do the sinner's prayer so them things can't get us."

"You can't be playing with God," said Pa Frank.

"Who's playing? I want to be saved and go to heaven when I die, and it wouldn't hurt to have some protection again them Godzilla creatures from hell. What does the bible say about how do we get saved?"

"Well, let me think. Mama used to say that we have to go by the Roman's road to salvation." Pa Frank rubbed his hand slowly through his gray straggly beard as he pondered. "Ok…Yea…Let's see. Romans 3: 23, Romans 6: 23, and Romans 10: 9. Well, let me read it to you so that you will hear it straight from the bible."

CHAPTER THREE

A New World Order

Revelation 6: 14-17

14. And the heaven departed as a scroll when it is rolled together; and every mountain and island were moved out of their places.

15. And the kings of the earth, and the great men and the rich men, and the chief captains, and the mighty men, and every bondman, and every free man, hid themselves in the dens and in the rocks of the mountains.

16. And said to the mountains and rocks, Fall on us, and hide us from the face of him that sits on the throne, and from the wrath of the Lamb;

17. For the great day of his wrath is come; and who shall be able to stand?

The whole world was in total chaos; some nations were on fire-nuclear plants had exploded and wipe out entire cities; most of Iraq and half of Syria, Jordan and parts of Saudi Arabia were destroyed by Iraq's nuclear bomb exploding upon itself even before launching. Those nations of the world looked like a wasteland-they had plundered back into the Ice Age.

There was no safety anywhere. All were affected by this unknown cataclysmic storm. It was a jungle now where only the strong survived and plagued the weak and venerable. There was weeping, weeping, and more weeping; all wept for somebody or something.

Jerusalem that has the Wailing Wall, was now a wailing city engulfed by grief; filled with tears that could not be easily wiped away. All youth and innocence had been snatched away without notice.

Nothing made sense anymore. Supermarkets had no food; the shelves were empty everywhere. The gas stations had no gas; cars and trucks were stopped on the side of the road, and even still on the road; and hospitals simply had no more room for anyone; patients were even lined down the halls-many dying. They had run out of medication which was already low-no more morphemes, no demurral, no sedatives, no valium, nothing for pain, or for anxiety, just nothing. Nurses and doctors were overwhelmed; many of them just ran out of the hospital feeling helpless and hopeless.

The United States was rocking and reeling with disaster just as well. No longer the world super power; it too struggled in this unexplained cataclysmic storm that blanketed the entire globe. No internet, no cell phones, and very little electricity. Those things that they had taken for granted were now taken away-even fresh running water in the homes was stopped.

The rich and wealthy were not spared either; their money, fame, and status made no difference-but they still expected some degree of favor, but there was none to be given-even if they wanted to.

The League of Nations, The United Stations, The European Union, and a host of national leaders from around the world had an emergency meeting in Rome Italy. This was one time that they had to put aside their differences and come together to save the world-either live together or die apart; there was no other options.

Even amidst the sovereign meeting of the minds of the world, Rome simmered and burned outside. Tragedy ran rampantly through this antique city like hungry hyenas chasing their prey. Yes, that great city that once ruled the world; that produced great leaders as Julius Caesar, Caesar Augustus, Trajan, and Constantine the Great was now physically knocked to its knees and searching for hope.

People crowded the streets outside the Vatican, lying prostrate weeping and praying that the Pope had an answer for them, that he could somehow save them out of this wretched state of suffering.

Nobody wanted to openly say it, but secretly, they all hoped that the church could save them, or at the very least, show them a way out-that's why they chose Rome, the heart of the Christian church.

They met and discussed while the world was forever changed.

In the United States of America, Key West was now gone and washed away; the ocean shore line now rested in Miami; New Orleans Louisiana had also succumbed to the might of the sea; its levies were now breached forever; Like the famous city of Atlantis, it now lay silently under water-becoming a graveyard for its citizens; parts of New York and all down the east coast was submerged in the sea, and the west coast was not spared either; half of Los Angeles lay succumbed to the Pacific Ocean, and there was no more Central America; it too had vanished into the ocean-no more connection between North and South America; Millions had drowned around the world. Earth had shifted out of its resting place.

The nations agreed that they could not operate as they had in the past. There needed to be one leader, one man as supreme president of the entire world who had insight and foresight enough to reestablish some kind of order amidst this pervasive pandemonium; someone that could lead them out and back to normalcy, though it had obviously changed forever; and someone whose eloquent enough to explain what had happened to the world, and where was all of the missing love ones.

"Gentlemen, it is our duty to reestablish some degree of order to what's left of us. We don't rightly know what has happened, but it has come home to all of us." The leader from South Africa said, with a deep accent as he motioned around the room. "We are all affected by this-whatever it is, aliens or what. We are forever changed. Today, we must choose a supreme leader of the world, and give our complete allegiance to him. Our subjects have to see some strength in us, or we shall all perish together. Who knows whether the aliens or whatever will return to take the rest of us."

"I agree." The leader from England interjected. "We must choose today before we go back to our own counties. People are hurting everywhere. Let us choose amongst ourselves this day, and let us not leave without a chosen leader, and if you do not agree, do it for the whole of us. Humanity is in jeopardy this day. We need a leader; let us choose so when we leave here, we know who to follow and who to turn to."

"We need help!" The President of Nigeria Shouted at all of them.

"What's new? Y'all have always begged for help." Another yelled out, hidden in the crowd.

"Who said that?" He shouted back; his angry eyes shooting through the crowd. "How can you be so evilly sarcastic in a time like this?"

"Gentlemen, gentlemen, shall we not keep our wits about us this day; if not for us, but for the hurting masses that dawn our doors and our streets. If ever there was a time that we needed leadership, it is right now on these painful shores. As the great writer John Dunne once said, No man is an island off to himself, every man is a part of the main; if my brother dies, it diminishes me. So, ask not for whom the bell tolls; the bell tolls for thee. The bell of society, even humanity tolls for us. We must rise up beyond our fears and uncertainty and embrace right now, what has happened, and where we are around The Globe. Morn for yesterday, but tackle head on this new day. The people are looking to us for leadership and answers, and we shall find them. But we will recover and rebuild a new life, and it starts right here." Abu Nebuchez spoke long and eloquently to the statesmen; polished from a child for this day to be such a leader. The world leaders sat mesmerized by his words, and astonished at how composed he was in such a time. "If chosen to be this world leader, I will bring back peace around the world. It shall be my first objective. I already have a plan; of those plans, the first thing that we must do is reestablish electricity around the world so that we can direct the masses by television, internet, and all the mechanism that we can muster. They are like sheep that need a shepherd; like cattle that need a herdsman. They are looking to us. IF we panic, they too will panic; if we walk out of this room afraid and frightened, they too shall remain afraid and frightened. No, this is a time of peace, global peace- A time of reckoning."

Abu Nebuchez, from a little unknown city nestled in the sun scorched hills between Iraq and Iran, spoke for nearly two hours, easing their fears and calming their nerves. He too was highly educated with a Ph.D in psychology, political science, and law. He stood erect with broad shoulders and an air of arrogance that announced him. Abu Nebuchez was raised and groomed all of his life for such a time as this. Destiny had come knocking on his front door, and he readily answered.

For a short while, Abu Nebuchez brought peace to the world as all tried to restructure their lives, at home and abroad. They thought that they were slowly putting their lives back together again; and although they missed their missing loved ones, they had to go one with life-such that it was; and for a while, it worked, but then war broke out everywhere-one nation against another, and many wanted to dethrone Abu Nebuchez, but he had become just too powerful with most of the world following him while the rest of the world watched and mourned.

Abu Nebuchez soon ruled the whole world with war everywhere against those that refuse to submit to his rule; and nations around the world rose up against each other-all wanted to rule and not become a part of Abu Nebuchez one world leadership system.

Many were dying by the masses everywhere, and all that did not die from war, died from sickness, disease, hunger or thirst. There was just not enough food or water to supply everyone. A great many of the fish in the sea were dead because the waters had turned to blood or wormwood (doctors and scientist were baffled. They just could not figure out why the water was turning to blood and wormwood); thousands upon thousands of fish lay dead along the shores. Men and women dead bodies lay along the streets everywhere, and many stiff corpses still left in houses waiting to be buried-just too many dead to bury. The stench of death blanketed the streets like molten ash from an angry volcano.

In spite of the pervasively wondering death, Abu Nebuchez refused to relinquish power or any of his post; they would serve him or die. There was no other alternative; so the world fought and fought and fought as hate rested in men's bosom like poison serpent.

CHAPTER FOUR

The Locus

Revelation 9: 1-11

1. And the fifth angel sounded, and I saw a star fall from heaven unto the earth: and to him was given the key of the bottomless pit.

2. And he opened the bottomless pit; and there arose a smoke out of the pit, as the smoke of a great furnace; and the sun and the air were darkened by reason of the smoke of the pit.

3. And there came out of the smoke locusts upon the earth; and unto them was given power, as the scorpions of the earth have power.

4. And it was commanded them that they should not hurt the grass of the earth, neither any green thing, neither any

tree; but only those men which have not the seal of God in their foreheads.

5. And to them it was given that they should not kill them, but that they should be tormented five months: and their torment was as the torment of a scorpion, when he strikes a man.

6. And in those days shall men seek death, and shall not find it; and shall desire to die, and death shall flee from them.

7. And the shapes of the locusts were like unto horses prepared unto battle; and on their heads were as it were crowns like gold, and their faces were as the faces of men.

8. And they had hair as the hair of women, and their teeth were as the teeth of lions.

9. And they had breastplates, as it were breast plates of iron; and the sound of their wings was as the sound of chariots of many horses running to battle.

10. And they had tails like unto scorpions, and there were things in their tails: and their power was to hurt men five months.

11. And they had a king over them, which is the angel of the bottomless pit, Abaddon, but in the Greek tongue his name is Apollyon." After reading that bible passage, Willie looked up at V and slowly uttered, hardly parting his lips. "Them things are here to torture anybody that's not saved."

The candy-apple red mustang eased up along the curve adjacent to Willie's church. Its engine rumbled like an irritated lion awakened from his sleep. V was afraid to drive into the church parking lot. Half of the windows in the church were shattered with flayed glass scattered across the pavement.

Dark grey smoke eased up to the angry sky from the rear of the building while streaked torn asphalt covered the ground like an earthquake had shaken it apart.

People were on the streets all around the church, though they were not concerned about the church itself; they were just trying to console one another as best they could while trying to make sense of what had happened.

A grandmother bellowed out in despair for her missing grandbabies, while her daughters wept uncontrollably on anybody's shoulder that would bear her. Emotional pain blanketed the crowd like a sworn of flies resting on a dead caucus.

V just sat there staring at the church, lost in a vale of bitter sweet thoughts of her beloved Snow. She prayed softly as she had never prayed before; trying to bargain with God on her beloved's behalf. She remembered the last time she saw him with fire red eyes and three sixes burned in his hand. She could still smell the stench of chard burning flesh.

She eased her head onto the steering wheel, enveloped by a thousand thoughts of what might be, and what should have been.

"You alright V?" Willie asked, trying to look at V and watch the church at the same time. "I know this is my church, but I think that we ought to get out of here while we still can. V, I got a bad feeling about this- A real bad feeling; and Snow probably ain't even in there. I don't see nobody moving around in there. And, I don't want to be here if hell breaks loose again."

"Willie just hush will you; just hush." She moaned in Willie's direction. "Just hush for a minute. I need to think."

"Sure, just take as long as you like," said Willie sarcastically. "I got to die someday anyway; might as well be here at my church."

"Willieeee!" She rolled her eyes at him.

V grabbed the steering wheel with both hands and squeezed it with all of her might while screaming into the air.

"V, now don't go snapping right now girl. I need you all here. You hear me? I need you all here. I don't know what we are up against, but we got to fight this together. I was just lying about not caring about living. I ain't in no hurry to die. When the Lord comes for me, I am going kicking and screaming; everybody gone know that I don't want to go. But, don't get me wrong now, I want to go to heaven, just not no time soon."

"Will you just shut up? What do you mean; you don't know what's happening. You're the only person that doesn't know Willie!" V said peering angrily into Willie's scary eyes as angry tears of desperation raced down her cheeks. "And you supposed to be a preacher! Didn't you preach this stuff every Sunday? You should be telling me what to do, and what to expect, and what's next. How do we survive this Willie? Huh, how do we come out of this?"

"Yea, I pastored, but like a lot of them, it was just a job for me. I was a hypocrite when it came to Christianity; Just a low down hypocrite V that was doing it for a check every week, but since this here happened and I got left behind, I gave my life to Jesus. I don't know what's going to happen next, but I know it ain't gone be good; that's why I say let's keep moving."

"Keep moving where Willie? Where we gone go? Haven't you heard? This thing, or whatever it is, happened everywhere, all over the world. There is no running from it, or starting over." V said amidst labored breaths.

"I know; I know...but...but...but." Willie stammered to say while staring off over V's shoulder into the distance.

"What? What is it Willie?" V asked swirling around to see what had engulfed Willie's attention.

Off in the distance, hanging low to the ground and stretched out from one end of the horizon to the other, it looked like a large black cloud was rushing their way. It would soon be upon them in no time.

"What is it Willie? Is it just blowing smoke from a fire in the next town?" V said nervously while resting her hands over her chest.

"I don't know V, but I know it ain't smoke, and it's not good for us. We better get out of here right now."

The black cloud raced closer and closer, now with a deep heavy rustling noise with it. The closer it got, the louder it became. An unbearable noise of, what it now seemed like millions upon millions of some kind of insects-large insect.

"Oh god, Willie what are we going to do? What are we gone do?" V screamed, still staring at the ominously approaching swarm of angry insects.

"Let's go V! Let's go before it is too late! I don't know what it is, but it can't mean us good. Let's go girl; let's go!" Willie shouted, never taking his eyes off of the approaching black cloud of unholy beasts.

V shifted the mustang into first gear and slammed on the gas pedal as hard as she could. They zoomed down the road, but it was too late. A massive swarm of strange looking insects blanketed the car-buzzing and rumbling all the time.

It sounded like big rocks or iron pellets were pounding the car. She couldn't see, so she slammed on brakes. Having no time to put on his seatbelt, Willie's head slammed against the hard dashboard of the car.

Like iron drops of rain plummeting the car, these strange ungodly insects covered the car from one end to the other. People were hollering and streaming everywhere. Their pain riddled terror filled screams filled the air and blanketed the whole town.

V could barely peer through her window and see that the creatures had completely covered some of the victims from head to toe. She thought that they were eating them alive.

"Oh god, oh god, Willie what should we do?" V yelled over at Willie in fear and desperation. "What are those things? Don't let them in here! Please God help us!"

"Right now, He's the only one that can help us, but I don't think that He will. If I remember correctly, those creatures are a part of our damnation, or salvation, depending on whose side you are on." Willie eased out, now getting a good look at the creatures.

V stared through the windshield at the creatures as they crawled all over her windshield and stared hungrily back at her-hissing as though trying to say something.

The creatures looked like overgrown locust-about two feet long; they had the body of a muscular horse with a long scorpion tail curled up over their backs with a glistening dagger protruding from it. They had the head of a man with a crown on it and long blond hair that draped down to their breast. The creatures seemed to hiss in harmony with long teeth hanging from their mouths as saliva splashed the grown before them. They were simply terrifying to behold.

The people outside the car were yet screaming in languishing pain. The locust stung and bit them over and over again on their entire body; whatever flesh that they could get to, they bit and stung over and over again. Yet, no one was dying; they just kept on screaming and hollering in agonizing pain.

One woman ran down the street, trying to get away, but she carried the stinging locust with her. They clung to her hair with stingers in her head and every place that they could get to; when she opened her mouth to scream, a locust jump in and stung her tongue and face and slid down her throat. She grabbed her neck and tried to scream, but nothing came out. Her neck swelled up twice its size-looking like it would explode in a minute. She fell to the ground, and more locust swarmed her until you could not see her at all, just a big ball of locust tearing into something.

A man stumbled profusely while covered by those horrible little loathsome beasts. His eyes had been gouged out by their poisonous stingers, but they still bit and stung his sockets as warm rich red blood ran violently covered her body.

Another man, while the locust continued their quest of diabolical pain, pulled his revolver from his pocket and put it to his head and pulled the trigger. Brain matter rocketed from the other side of his head as the bullet tore out. He wanted to end his suffering, but, even with a large gaping hole in his head, he still remain conscious and screamed even more because the locust were now inside of the gaping bullet hole stinging and biting his warm draining flesh.

Several people, both men and women, ran through the church, up the stairwell to the steeple trying to escape the locust, but it was no use; they followed them, biting and stinging as they went. They got to the roof of the church, locust still stinging, still biting, and all of them leaped off of the roof-three stories up, but no one died; they all hit the pavement with a hard loud thud with broken arms, broken legs, and broken necks, but nobody died; they just tried to stumble away in their now mutilated state.

"Oh god, Willie this is horrible, just horrible. What are we going to do? They are everywhere!" V said, looking all around them in terror. "Thank god they can't get into this car with us… thank god."

"Oh they can get in if they wanted to. Trust me; they're not interested in us. I accepted the Lord as my savior, and if they're not interested in you, then somewhere, you have too."

"I did, a couple of days ago, but I hadn't gone to church." She said.

"It ain't about going to church; it's about knowing Him and accepting Jesus as your personal savior. You have done that haven't you V."

"Yes of course; I told you that. I did it a few days ago." V said. "But what are they? Where did they come from?"

"You got a bible in here?" Willie asked, looking around the car.

"Yes, one is in my bag. An old lady gave it to me a few days ago. The one that sold me this car. Why?"

Willie scramble through V's back pack and finally found the old beat up time riddled bible.

"Why you need that?"

"If I am right, it's going to tell us what these creatures are." Willie spoke as he opened the bible and frantically flipped through its pages-some stuck together, beaten by time. "Yea, yea, here it is."

"What?" She asked, trying to contain herself while looking at the loathing creatures that covered her car, and tortured the people outside. "What does it say? Huh? Read it. Read it Willie-hurry up….Oh God, what are we going to do?"

"Ok…Ok, here we go. I got it." Willie yelled out amidst excitement.

"Read it." V said, trying to turn away and not look those hideous creatures in the eyes.

"Revelation nine and one through eleven says," shaking in fear, he started to read aloud while sweat ran down his face and covered his shaking hands. "1. And the fifth angel sounded, and I saw a star fall from heaven unto the earth: and to him was given the key of the bottomless pit.

2. And he opened the bottomless pit; and there arose a smoke out of the pit, as the smoke of a great furnace; and the sun and the air were darkened by reason of the smoke of the pit.

3. And there came out of the smoke locusts upon the earth; and unto them was given power, as the scorpions of the earth have power.

4. And it was commanded them that they should not hurt the grass of the earth, neither any green thing, neither any tree; but only those men which have not the seal of God in their foreheads.

5. And to them it was given that they should not kill them, but that they should be tormented five months: and their torment was as the torment of a scorpion, when he strikes a man.

6. And in those days shall men seek death, and shall not find it; and shall desire to die, and death shall flee from them.

7. And the shapes of the locusts were like unto horses prepared unto battle; and on their heads were as it were crowns like gold, and their faces were as the faces of men.

8. And they had hair as the hair of women, and their teeth were as the teeth of lions.

9. And they had breastplates, as it were breast plates of iron; and the sound of their wings was as the sound of chariots of many horses running to battle.

10. And they had tails like unto scorpions, and there were things in their tails: and their power was to hurt men five months.

11. And they had a king over them, which is the angel of the bottomless pit, Abaddon, but in the Greek tongue his name is Apollyon." After reading that bible passage, Willie looked up at V and slowly uttered, hardly parting his lips. "Them things are here to torture anybody that's not saved."

"Didn't it say something about a mark on our foreheads or something?" V quickly whipped.

"Yea." Willie replied, looking wide eyed at the creatures.

"Well, do you see any mark on my forehead," said V, pulling her hair back. "Well, is any marks on my forehead Willie?"

"Nawl, I don't see anything." Willie stared hard at V's forehead, hoping to see something. "Maybe only God and the creatures can see the mark I guess."

"Well look harder Willie! You ain't looking hard enough!" She franticly shouted at Willie.

"Do you see anything on my forehead?" Willie shouted back, moving in closer to V, hoping that she would see something.

"No, only sweat. Did you receive The Lord?"

"You know I did, but V looks like we're in trouble cause those things are acting differently. Look like they're all focused on us. Lord Jesus please help us." Willie screamed up to heaven with arms outstretched.

The locust started piling onto the car, almost as if they were commanded to. The loud noise became deafening. V and Willie held their hands over their ears and prayed to God, no, begged God to save them; for they knew that it was just a matter of time before the windshield caved in-then they would experience the anguish suffering that the people outside was going through.

Many of the people's eyes were swollen shut, and their lips and ears were about to burst. They just moaned and groaned in agony as the locust continued their quest.

"I guest this is it V," said Willie as he grabbed her hand and squeezed softly. "They will be in here in a minute."

"Not without a fight. I'll go out fighting." V said, pulling two 9mm out of her backpack, and then pulling the hammer back preparing to fire. "Bring it. Come onnnn!"

"You really think you have a chance against all of those creatures? What? You gone kill about nine of them? V, look, it's a billion of those things out there." Willie reasoned. "Prayer is the only chance we got. Put those guns down and pray. Pray like you've never prayed before!"

"Well, that will be nine less than what they had." She stared profusely at the blond haired hideous locust while she held the guns stiffly.

Willie nervously got one of the guns and just held it in his lap.

"I feel stupid." He struggled to say amidst nervous breaths.

"Not as stupid as you're going to feel when those things start chumping on you for dinner."

The glass cracked and streaked from one end to the other, readying to break. Willie shut his eyes tight and started praying out loud.

V thought to shoot before the glass broke, to go out as she pleased-defiant to the end.

Suddenly Morrow appeared- the angel that had been bound to earth because he had gotten too close to Snow and the other humans that he was charged to look after with the least bit of interference. The locust leaped from the car and swarmed on him, covering him from head to toe.

"That was Morrow! Morrow...Morrow! Oh god, they got Morrow Willie; they got Morrow." V screamed with her hands covering her mouth, and tears streaming down her cheeks.

"Well, let's get out of here while they are focusing on him." Willie reached for the door handle.

"We can't just leave him. He is the one that saved us at the church, remember." V whipped.

Morrow moaned softly and flinched hard, and all of the locust fail off of him and lay upon the ground.

"Really? I mean really. " Morrow said, looking off into the distance. "Did you really think that I could be so easily conquered by your beastly children?" He spoke into the air as if someone was listening.

The clouds in the sky rushed and rolled up like a scroll while lightening raced and streaked, and flashed across the beaming sky. The winds blew and howled like a wailing old lady that had lost the last of her children.

Suddenly, an invisible force hit the ground like a bomb had exploded-leveling some of the building, and violently tossing people like little rag dolls everywhere while the glowing sun eased back behind the distant mountains and refused to send light for a moment; even pushing V's car a few yards over and slamming it against another car. Dust blazed up everywhere and then slowly eased back onto its place on the ground from whence it had come.

The locust stood still and silently at attention like soldiers awaiting command.

When the dust finally cleared, there stood regally an angel clothed in radiant white apparel with locks of long curly white hair and a long white beard that lay supremely between the bronze pectoral muscles in his chest.

"Ah yea, Apollyon, my brother from down under-the bottomless pit. You always did know how to make a grand entrance." Morrow said sarcastically. "Did you really think that your pets could harm me?"

"No, but then, well, you are almost human, and I owe you, remember," said Apollyon, rubbing his long slender fingers through his long white beard that lay softly upon his chest. "I couldn't resist, seeing that it's been such a long time, but I keep up; news travel fast about you- even in the underworld. An angel whose wings the Old Man clipped. Hah, wouldn't want to be you, but then, I never did."

"Well, I figured that you would show up sooner or later with your posse; and it ain't that bad once you get use to these earthlings-they're alright." Morrow said peering back at Apollyon with no fear.

"How can you say that about a piece of clay that ain't no more than a hunk of talking dust that will soon return back to dust. They're like rodents that's always taking and littering." Apollyon whipped angrily back at Morrow.

"Yea, but The Almighty favors them." Morrow replied, strolling his fingers through his short cropped beard.

"Yea, but I don't see how He could put so much value in a piece of walking, talking dust. I just don't get it." Apollyon whipped. "If I had my way, I'd be done with them all."

"But you don't have your way; now do you?" Morrow said with a hint of a smirk.

"For a little while I do." He chuckled, rubbed his hand through his long white beard again, and then raised his head high in arrogance. "And, I shall cherish every torturing moment of it."

Apollyon raised his right hand, motioning to his creatures; then, like a whirlwind, they were all off and gone.

People were still crying and screaming; some of them even looked up towards heaven, shook their fist, and cursed God for allowing those creatures to torment them. Everybody was swollen; black and blue wounds with yellow pulse oozing from them, covered their bodies, but nobody died. Death refused to take them.

Morrow casually walked over to V's car, pulled the door open and motioned for them to get out.

"Now that's what um talking bout! That's what um talking bout!" Willie yelled as he leaped from the car in excitement. "Come back here again, and we gone whip y'all butt worse than this next time!" He shouted into the sky in the direction that he thought the locust and Apollyon had gone.

V leaped into Morrow's arms crying. She horrified and trembling all over. She felt good to be held in a man's arms, and let all of her worries and cares fall on his masculine shoulders. For the first time in her life, she wanted to yield and bath in all of her femininity and let a man be the man for her; if only for this one time. She needed a strong shoulder to rest her weary head on.

"And what about Snow?" She asked with tears in her eyes, afraid of what she might here of what had befallen her beloved.

CHAPTER FIVE

The Angelic storm

Revelation 10: 1-3

1. And I saw another mighty angel come down from heaven, clothed with a cloud: and a rainbow was upon his head and his face was as it were the sun, and his feet as pillars of fire;

2. And he had in his hand a little book open; and he set his right foot upon the sea, and his left foot on the earth,

3. And cried with a loud voice, ass when a lion roars; and when he had cried, seven thunders uttered their voices.

The sky glistened and sparkled in a land far away from nowhere, unlike anywhere, in a land somewhere between the hymnals of time-caught up between man's reality and the celestial shores of the divine; there sat amidst ambiguous ambitions wrapped up in sultry pretention, a host of angels begrudging the times.

They came together for two reasons: to lavish this time of man's judgement and punishment brought forth by The Father of all creation-The supreme being, God of all; and too, once and for all, destroy Morrow (the angel that had been clipped of his wings and made to dwell on earth like a mere mortal man) before he returned back to his original angelic role of power-only matched by the great archangel Gable; for they knew that after all that they had done to him during his time of clay, he would, no doubt, return their cruelty and unleash much more than they wanted to bear. Yes, they had to get rid of Morrow or forever look over their shoulders for his eminent retribution.

They sat stealthy in a white marble room; everything in it was gleaming white and clad in white with a few hints of vibrant colors here and there; they rested on golden glistening chairs while softly conversing with each other, but, it was more than apparent and even obvious that they were uneasy about their anticipated eminent endeavors.

There, sitting around the white marble table were: Pergamos, angel of fear; Trusious, angel of lust; Thadeous, angel of anger; Alglea, angel of vanity; Adrasteia, angel of beauty; Alexander, angel of depression; Lambeer, angel of hate; Sheena, angel of pleasure; Ericleates, angel of war; Laodecius, angel of the grave; Ericdotus, angel of death, and a host of other angels in attendance, but too cautious to show their faces, for none of them were quick to consider irritating Gable, but all of them wanted a piece of Morrow.

"Ah kmmmm!" Thadeous cleared his throat, beckoning for their attention. "Now we all know why we are here. The question then becomes how do we accomplish our mission."

"And exactly what is that?" Pergamos eased out. "So that we will all be on the same page here."

"We all know what we are here for: to celebrate the fall of the earthlings, and to destroy our mutual enemy, Morrow, our former prince." Thadeous whipped out in his usual angry tone.

"But gentlemen, need I remind you all what happened when we last made such an attempt on prince Morrow?" Alglea said, rubbing her hands through her long curly ebony locks of hair. "Gable came to his rescue. We could have all been destroyed, but the prince spared us. I don't think that he will be so kind if he catches us in a second attempt. So, we must consider, are we ready to do a futile battle against Gable-I don't think so; for none can stand against him and absorb his wrath."

"Alglea, as usual, you always think only of yourself, but then, that's what makes you vanity-huh? But, he won't. I made sure of it. Gable is for away dealing with situations in the Far East; trying to protect those that the Father has marked and favored as His own. He will be too busy to concern himself with the salvation of Morrow."

"But, this is Gable that we are talking about. He could be anywhere in an instant." Lambeer snapped as he looked around the table into all of their eyes. I agree with Alglea, Gable's mercy saved us the last time, but the prince might not be so merciful again; and you know that a great many of angels are waiting to take our places. So, all that I am saying brothers are for us to think long and hard before we attempt this, for prince Gable seems to lean in favor of Morrow; don't know why, but he does."

They all shuffled in their seats uncomfortably around the table, knowing full well that what Lambeer said was painfully true.

"Um out," said Pergamos, angel of fear. "I don't fight battles that I know that I can't win."

"Me too," said Alexander, angel of depression.

They both simply disappeared like a whiff of smoke in the air; their golden chairs gleamingly empty.

Thadeous stared hard at the empty chairs that Pergamos and Alexander had just left, and then, he slammed his fist hard onto the marble table, cracking it with ease; then, suddenly, a piece of the table fail to the floor.

"I am fully in; I need no further persuasion. I owe Morrow, and it's time that I repay him for his previous callous misgivings towards me." Laodecius, angel of the grave interjected. "There be countless souls that he took from me. Yes, I am in. I want to see the look on his face when he realize that it is I coming back to reap revenge upon him. That is priceless.....Yessss, priceless."

"Me too, it might be fun, and it will definitely be more than exciting." Ericdotus, angel of the grave interjected. "Sometimes it gets a little boring in the underworld."

Suddenly, a gentle breeze eased through the room, stirring the colorful flowers nestled in their vases. It appeared as though a worm hole slowly twirling about unraveled while filled with many radiant colors, had appeared and expanded itself. Hope, the princess angel of love, gracefully stepped out with all of the splendor and grace of a queen endowed to rule.

"What is this?" Thadeous snapped at Hope. "You were not invited to this meeting, nor are you welcomed right now. Who told you of this gathering? I knew you to be too weak for such an undertaking as this. Go spread your mushy stuff somewhere else."

Hope perused the room, gleaming intently into all the other angels' eyes-hoping that they would realize futility of this endeavor, and the price that each of them would have to pay if caught.

"Do you really think that you all can succeed in this unholy, unrighteous endeavor that Thadeous proposes to you?" Hope asked them, as she gestured gently with her hands. "If I know of your meeting, don't you think that Gable also knows? And, you do know that Morrow and Gable are close, and if he didn't spare Morrow, I dare to think what he will do to you all. Where can you go that he cannot get to you, or what other angels will fight with you? Morrow will be restored sooner or later; you cannot alter that. It is in the Father's hands; but, please brothers and sisters don't destroy yourselves trying to destroy someone else; else you inherit the fate that befell the once archangel Lucifer-as all of you know so well. And, I dare not think that you want to incur the wrath of The Almighty Father. Gable is the least of your problems. Do you really want to take the chance of being destroyed forever, or changed into a demon like our other angels that revolted and followed Lucifer because he thought that he could dethrone The Father? Think my fellow angels-think for yourselves."

Thadeous fumed and hissed with eyes full of hate and madness, for he saw that Hope had touched most of them and made them doubt their intentions.

While Thadeous pondered his next move, the marble door to the room silently eased opened and a hush permeated the room as all of them gazed at the mammoth of a figure gracing their presence. He was tall with broad shoulders that an airplane could land on. His head tilted high in pride and arrogance, he stood in the doorway erect with his long silky white hair laying softly upon his shoulders while he looked over the room of celestials. It was Apollyon; the angel of the bottomless pit that he and his locust beasts had been release just recently to torment the humans.

"Well, this meeting gets more interesting by the minute." Hope said, with a smirk smile spread on her face. She looked again at Thadeous. "Need I say more, or do you need a planet to fall on your head dear prince of anger? Apollyon knows of this meeting. Do you really think that Gable doesn't know, or even Morrow for that matter."

He slammed his fist on the table, and looked out across the room and beyond, expecting someone else to come through the door.

CHAPTER SIX

No escape

Revelation 12: 1-4

1. And there appeared a great wonder in heaven; a woman clothed with the sun, and the moon under her feet; and upon her head, a crown of twelve stars;

2. And she being with child cried, travailing in birth and pained to be delivered.

3. And then appeared another wonder in heaven; and behold a great red dragon, having seven heads and ten horns, and seven crowns upon his heads.

4. And his tail drew the third part of the stars of heaven, and did cast them down to the earth: and the dragon stood before the woman which was ready to be delivered, for to devour her child as soon as it was born.

Jahbo, the Jamaican drug lord, drove his 600S Mercedes as fast as it would go, peeling screaming rubber as he went. His two men sat in the back seat peering out of the back window with terror written all over their faces, for they had seen what the locust had done to a few other folks. He zoomed around one curve after another, knocking over trach cans and mailboxes as he went. Jahbo could barely control the car, but he couldn't slow down, no, he refused to even consider slowing down no matter what the cost.

A swarm of locusts kept chasing them, right on their tales; every now and then, a few of them would catch up and plummet onto the the trunk of the car, trying to get in before the wind blew them off.

"You'd better speed up man! They catching up! Speed up man; speed up!" One of the Jamaicans, in terror and desperation, yelled at Jahbo from the back seat as his head slammed hard against the door window after Jahbo whipped hard around yet another curve.

"I am trying. Just shut up; we'll reach the safe house in a minute." Jahbo yelled back at them. "Just shut up and keep watching them!"

"I am just going to shoot the back glass out and kill a lot of them."

"No, no, don't do that you fool. You'll doom all of us; that window is what's keeping them off of us!" Jahbo hollered out in fear and desperation again.

He grasped the steering wheel and made a hard right turn onto Martin Luther King Junior Avenue; almost losing control of the car, he drove over a few signs while trying to regain control of the car.

The sun was setting fast and rushing back to the west to its nocturnal resting place. No one was on the streets; it was like a ghost town whose inhabitants had long died. The streets were deserted because they could only relieve themselves of the locusts if they stayed inside-windows shut tight and doors locked-no cracks or crevasses anywhere- particularly at night. The dark was always the most terrible times; they could hear screams bellow in the air and down the wanton streets.

"We are almost there; we're almost there fellows." Jahbo yelled out as he turned onto 6th street north, and roared over somebody's yard, leaving burrowed tire tracks on their green grass. He hit the remote button on his garage door opener and swerved into his driveway, barely missing the garage door. The Mercedes slammed into the back wall; Jahbo quickly pressed the down button. As the garage door finally shut, they could hear the locust slamming against the garage door, trying to get in.

Jahbo reached for the door handle to get out, but just before he could open the door, the garage burst into shaking and trembling violently. He thought that it was the locusts breaking in. The roof fell in; crashing down hard upon the black Mercedes. Jahbo could now see outside the garage amongst the dusk debris clouding the evening sky. He saw the other houses shaking violently out of their foundation-some even sinking into the earth. The oncoming evening shadows were filled with screams from people running out of their houses and into the clutches of the waiting locusts-they had to choose; be crushed or tormented by the locust. Their instincts wouldn't allow them to remain inside; they rushed from the house into the jaws and stingers of the loathsome locusts.

It seemed to last forever; houses, buildings, and businesses, along with people, were crumbling everywhere, and mother earth even opened her mouth wide and swallowed entire buildings and some entire streets were gone. The earth rocked and reeled from one end of the planet to the other. Tokyo Japan, Shanghai China, Delhi India, Cairo Egypt, Tehran Iran, and all the cities around the world were shaking from the earth quake. Most of the coastal cities and states lost even more of their land to the ocean.

Many men called on their gods, while others cursed God for bringing this, or for allowing it to be. Building crumbled upon people as they ran down the shaking streets with nowhere to go. Million upon millions were killed around the world, but mother earth refused to stop rocking and reeling around the globe-anything that could be shaken, was shaken.

"Aaahhhh, we're fixing to die! We're fixing to die! Oh god, I don't want to die like this." One of the Jamaicans in the back seat yelled out as the car sank lower and lower into the ground with most of the garage rubble on them. "Please…Please…Somebody help us… Help…Help!"

"Shut up fool…Shut up!" Jahbo yelled back at him again while letting the window down. "Let your windows down and let's crawl out of here."

Jahbo wiggled his way through the window of the fastly sinking car; his comrades followed suit. The earth still shook violently as they stumbled their way out of the rubble of the garage. Most of the houses were in shambles or completely underground with only the tops of their roofs showing.

The sky laid ominously red against the glowing moon as though God Himself was angry with them and was pouring out His wrath upon the earth.

Suddenly, they heard the sound of the locusts returning for them.

"Get back in the car! Get back in the car and roll up the windows-hurry!" Jahbo yelled to his men as he stumbled his way towards the car. "And roll up your windows when you get in-hurry! Better to die buried underground, than to die being those hideous things dinner."

All of them fell several times as they tried their very best to run for the car with a shaking earth under their feet. It was no use, the locust caught them, and began to sting, bite, and devour them. Their screams of horror, mixed with their useless fun fire, filled the air and mingled amongst the already screams of pain and suffering.

CHAPTER SEVEN

Abu Nebuchez fury

Revelation 11: 13-14

13. And the same hour was there a great earthquake, and the tenth part of the city fell, and in the earthquake were slain of men seven thousand: and the remnant were affrighted, and gave glory to the God of heaven.

14. The second woe is past; and, behold, the third woe comes quickly.

Amidst all of the chaos and pandemonium, Abu Nebuchez sat quietly in a corner with his arms folded, without any hints of fear, in his lavish office while the earth quaked violently beneath his feet.

Chandeliers fell from the ceiling and crashed to the marble floor into a thousand pieces, sending glass flying everywhere. His palace was crumbling all around him-walls colliding, floors opening up and swallowing furniture. There were yelling and screaming everywhere as many plunged to their deaths from higher floors, with some building crushing others. His servants ran about yelling and screaming in fear; they didn't know which way to go, or what to do; they had never experienced an earthquake in their small country, but Abu Nebuchez knew that it would soon end, and he would remain alive, in power, and still rule the whole world, but now he just had to ride it out; he felt that it was time to become tougher and ruthless upon those that would resist him-time to pull off the sheep clothing-which had become most uncomfortable now.

He knew the bible quite well; amongst his other earned degrees, he was also a Doctor of Theology-so he knew biblically what was to come next.

Suddenly, the ground finally stopped shaking, and after a little while, things stopped falling and settled down. Abu Nebuchez was covered in dust from his head to his feet.

Eskander, Abu Nebuchez personal assistant, the one that ran his office and directed everything and everybody around President Abu Nebuchez, ran into the office to make sure that the president was alright. Nobody saw the president without first going through Eskander, and for that, many of the army's generals and those in power, did not like him. It was as though Eskander was second in command without ever really being in command.

"Sire...Sire...Sire, are you alright? Are you alright Sire?" Eskander yelled as he ran toward Abu Nebuchez. "We must go to the underground right away, for we don't know what's happening next, or if another earthquake will soon come worse than this one. We must go sire. We must go!"

"Where is my phone Eskander? Find my phone." He said, rising to his feet. "Find my phone. I must check on the world. I suspect that this earthquake, no doubt, hit everywhere; I was expecting it."

"But sire, I must get you to safety."

"I am alright, and we shall go to the underground city, but right now, I need my phone." Abu Nebuchez insisted.

"But." Eskander started to say.

"No buts, get me a phone this instant!" Abu Nebuchez snapped loudly at Eskander.

Eskander whirled about, turned, and dashed off into the adjacent rumbled room; moments later, he returned with Abu Nebuchez cell phone in his hand.

"Your phone sire," said Eskander reaching the phone out to his lord. "Now let's be off; I've got the limousine waiting for you outside."

Abu Nebuchez started walking towards the door of his once lavish office, trying to knock the dust off of himself and make a call at the same time.

General Amad burst into the room, with several soldiers behind him, and rushed up to Abu Nebuchez in a haze of fire wrenching adrenalin.

"Sire, are you alright? Who struck us? We shall strike back harder; I've got the nuclear bombs on ready right now; just tell us where to aim and they are history. How dare they attack us."

"No, no, no, you cannot fire a bomb into the heavens. It would be of no purpose. It was a global earthquake." He said as he listened through the phone to the ringing number that he had just dial up.

"How you know this so quickly?" The General asked, startled. "They are probably getting ready to attack again, but only this time, they'll come with much more power."

Abu Nebuchez paused in the midst of his conversation and shot a menacing look at General Amad.

"I am the president, not you! Don't ever question me again or else it will be your last time!" President Abu Nebuchez said with penetrating eyes. "Are we clear on that?"

"Yes Sire. It will never happen again," said General Amad nervously.

"Just trust me, I know." He turned and shuffled through some books and disarrayed papers lying next to an overturned desk, he found a book and handed it to the general.

"What's this?" The General asked confused.

"It's the bible; you might want to read it, especially, the last book called Revelation. You'll be one step ahead of everyone else-or at least, ahead of the smart people that refuse to read such rhetoric. It tells you what will happen next."

"Huh, the bible, but we live by the Quran, Allah. We don't need no infidel's book." General Amad said, tasting his words very carefully.

"You speak dangerously General. If I were you, I'd be careful of any reference to that book...very careful." Abu Nebuchez stared at him hard as he spoke. "That is a book that is filled with what we can expect next."

The General dropped his head softly into the locks of his shoulders and waited for further commands from President Abu Nebuchez.

"Sire, we must go now; for some of your enemies might think this an opportunity to strike." Eskander blurted out amidst their conversation. He softly pulled Abu Nebuchez by the arm.

"Now there you go, as usual, poking your big pointed nose where it doesn't belong." The General said, rolling his eyes over at Eskander.

"And you had better be careful too, before you get hung and fed to the fowls of the air...If they will eat an old buzzard like you." Eskander snapped with an air of disrespect.

"Hello, hello, just checking in to see how did you all fare during this untimely horrific earthquake." Abu Nebuchez spoke loudly into the phone as though he had a bad phone reception.

"It's bad Mr. President, really really bad." The voice on the other end of the phone stumbled to say. "All around the world were hit hard and suffered millions of lives lost-Poland, Russia, Ukraine, Africa, Iran, Iraq, China, Japan, United States; you name any country around the world and they were hit by this devastating earthquake and even most of the islands were washed away. And, amongst all of this, we are still having to deal with those hideous locust swarming everywhere. It's bad Mr. President-real bad. What are we going to do? We don't have enough graves for all of the millions upon millions that have died." The voice cracked on the other end of the phone, genuinely concern.

"We'll just advise them to have mass graves and burn the bodies. That's all we can do. I am about to call a joint meeting with all my leaders around the world. We've got to restore some kind of order in the midst of all of this chaos." Abu Nebuchez said firmly.

"Just tell me where and when, and I'll be there Mr. President." The voice on the other end of the phone chimed.

"I'll get back to you when everything is set."

Abu Nebuchez hung up the phone with a snap.

"We must go now Sire; must not delay any longer." Eskander said, softly tugging on the Nebuchez arm.

Abu Nebuchez swiftly exited the room, walking briskly beside his assistant Eskander.

The General just stood there and gazed angrily at Eskander as they exited the room for an awaiting entourage to carry him to his underground hideaway.

CHAPTER EIGHT

The Last World War

Revelation 9: 13-16

13. And the sixth angel sounded, and I heard a voice from the four horns of the golden altar which is before God,

14. Saying to the sixth angel which had the trumpet, loose the four angels which are bound in the great river Euphrates'

15. And the four angels were loosed, which were prepared for an hour, and a day, and a month, and a year, for to slay a third part of man.

16. And the number of the army of horsemen were two hundred thousand thousand: and I heard the number of them.

A ferocious fiery mountain fell from the heavens and raced towards the earth with blinding speed while a glowing ablaze tail trailed closely behind it. Men could see it from around the globe; they stared up at the incoming burning mountain, and wondered where it would hit and who would survive.

This humongous mountain of fire zoomed across the sky as if God himself had thrown it forth from His celestial throne-angered at the ways of men that had become so utterly corrupted until even at this time of test, they still refused to amend their ways.

Pa Frank, Mr. Pocket, and Mr. Archie, stared up at the sky like everybody else did; They wondered what was it, and where would it land.

"Yawl know we can kiss ourselves goodbye, don't you?" Mr. Pocket said without ever taking his eyes off the sky. "I mean, wherever that thing lands, it's going to affect all of us… I guarantee it."

"Um…um…um scared." Mr. Archie eased out.

"Me too," said Pa Frank

"No, um scared for real; like Vietnam kind of scared." Mr. Archie eased out, voice slightly trembling.

"Ain't no need in getting scared now. Why yawl scared? Ain't you saved? Haven't you given your life to Christ? Why are you worried? Oh you of little faith. Ain't that's what Jesus asked His disciples when they were scared of the storm?" Mr. Pocket said, now gazing over at them. "You don't want to live in hell and then die and go to hell. Nawww, not me, I have decided to trust Him all the way up to the very end. I am a little nervous and concerned about that falling fire coming our way, but I ain't scared. God promised us that He would take care of us, so I am trusting Him at His Word."

"Well, ain't that something. Look whose quoting scriptures. You been reading-huh." Pa Frank said with a hint of humor.

"You better be reaing too." Mr. Pocket whipped back. "Oh, and don't worry bout that twenty five dollars you owe me-um good."

"Oh no, um not going into eternity owing anybody; why I'll owe you forever. No- sir- ree, here take it." Pa Frank said, reaching into his pocket and handed Mr. Pocket twenty five dollars.

"Lord help us. If there ever was a time that we needed a savior, it is right now."

After staring up at the racing falling burning mountain until their necks ached, they finally eased back into the old store, where by now, all three of them lived. They had no customers now-a-days, so all of their food, they rationed for themselves while they watched one another's back and protected each other during these brazen times where men had become more like animals in a jungle where only the strong survived by taking from the weak.

Mr. Pocket looked down the street at a family of Asians scuffling to move down to their basement. The elderly man was fussing at his wife and the younger children in a foreign language; obviously, lamenting them to make haste.

Even if the basement couldn't save them, they still had to do whatever they could to save their own lives-however futile it might seem.

"Look at them, poor thang; they really think that that basement is going to save them." Pocket said, staring over at them and shaking his head from side to side in bewilderment.

"Look Pocket, they just doing what they can. You can't blame them. If I didn't know any better, I'd be trying to hide too." Pa Frank said soberly. "But, I know that there is no place to hide from the wrath of God-either you already got Him or you don't, and I pity the people that don't."

At midnight, a few days later, the burning mountain crashed violently into the North Pacific Ocean with the force and power of a hundred neutron bombs- sending water and sea creatures hurling hundreds of miles up into the atmosphere. It made the nuclear bombs that the United States dropped on Hiroshima and Nagasaki look like child's play in comparison. The whole earth shook from one end to the other-all felt something from its violent crash; no continent was spared. It sent many 100 foot tidal waves racing for most Asian shores. Islands disappeared; mountains vanished in a moment.

All of Australia was under water and completely washed away like it had never been. South East Asia had vanished too, and most of China was completely flooded with its coastal cities now gone.

All coastal cities, around the world, were demolished-most completely gone with a hint of a new coast line. Grief and mourning spread from one end of the globe to the other-none was spared. One third of all the creatures in the sea were killed. Dead Sea creatures were floating upon the waters everywhere, and the stench of rotting flesh perused the air and reckoned the times. Most of the ships and boats in the sea, along with their sailors and crew, and captain were destroyed. This was a calamity unlike any that the people of the earth had ever experienced. They hadn't even had time to fully process the sudden loss of their loved ones, or the loathsome hideous scorpions- "people don't just disappear into the thin air." They kept questioning and moaning amongst themselves.

There were just too many dead bodies to have any individual funerals; so, in every city, they dug massive holes in the ground and bulldozed the dead into the holes; there were millions upon millions of bodies. Eventually, almost overcome by grief and the stench of death, they built public incinerators, like public mailboxes on the corner, to burn the dead- still, there were many bodies throughout the land, and the smell of death lingered in the air like the smell of a thousand kills waiting on swarming hungry vultures to devour them like a hungry lion's dinner.

China thought that war had been declared upon them, so they assembled a massive army of 200,000,000 soldiers to fight against the Westerners-The United States, their allies, and Israel. They hated the Westerners and particularly Israel. This was the beginning of World War three. Every nation took one side or the other-fight with someone or die alone.

The overwhelming fear of nuclear war hanged heavily over all nations head. One wrong move of one crazy president or General, and the whole world would become another Hiroshima and Nagasaki; only this time, there won't be any survivors.

"You know that you can't believe all of that stuff that you read on the internet or hear on T.V. Most of the time, they are just hyping thing up." Pa Frank said, looking over at Archie and Mr. Pocket. "You already know what the Bible says."

"Yea, but, I just like hearing it again from somebody else." Mr. Pocket said, looking back at Pa Frank.

"Well, I guess it's going to be what it's going to be; come hell or high water." Mr. Archie said, standing up and peering through the window to see what he could see.

Three of them talked and talked far into the night about what use to be, and the anticipation of what shall come to be. They had finally come to realize that life as they once knew it was now gone forever. They only had heaven or hell to look forward to, and nobody wanted to go to hell.

CHAPTER NINE

The Seal

Revelation 7: 1-3

1. And after these things I saw four angels standing on the four corners of the earth, holding the four winds of the earth, that the wind should not blow on the earth, nor on the sea, nor on any tree.

2. And I saw another angel ascending from the east, having the seal of the living God: and he cried with a loud voice to the four angels, to whom it was given to hurt the earth and the sea,

3. Saying, "Hurt not the earth, neither the sea, nor the trees, till we have sealed the servants lof our God in their foreheads.

V and Willie sat, in her candy apple red mustang, with their seats declined, top back, and stared up at the glowing stars refusing the dawn. They had been there for a few days; the falling fiery mountain had stopped everything, and everything that could float, had floated away.

The streets still had about a foot of water on them. The awful smell of decaying flesh still lingered in the air and invaded their nostrils like unwanted guess on a hot summer's night. Several death squads, as they were referred to (the men that went from street to street gathering up the dead and taking them to be incinerated) filed down every street with hordes of the dead waiting to be burned.

It was as though time itself had paused for a moment between its celestial hymnals, and given V and Willie a moment of rest; a moment to reflect and dream upon what use to be, and wish upon what seemingly should be, and even try to spiritually atone for their habit of sin filled ways. They just lay there and dreamed and wished amongst the twinkling disappearing stars.

"How can such a peaceful night be filled with so much pain? It has been such a nightmare?" V moaned still staring up at the vanishing stars. "I just feel so numb; just so numb. I don't know what to do, or what I am supposed to do. Nothing makes sense anymore Willie. I mean Snow is gone and the whole world is crazy. We've been attacked by monster locusts, earthquakes, a burning falling mountain, and now another world war. What's next? I mean really, what's next?"

Willie peered hard over at V, hoping that she didn't notice his stare, and wondered how to comfort her; although he himself was struggling emotionally too, he had to be strong- Strong enough for V to lean on at this uncertain time. He tasted his words very carefully before speaking- still looking over at V. Suddenly, he thought of how pretty she was, even with dirty clothes on and a raggedy scarf tied around her head. She was still a woman to behold.

V just sat there gazing up at the velvety sky, now softly humming to herself some melody from yesterday.

Swiftly Willie reached over and pulled her into his bosom and held her tightly with her head lying gently on his shoulder. V whimpered softly and wanted to pull away, but she couldn't; her wanton flesh wouldn't allow her to. It felt good being nestled in the masculine arms of a testosterone filled man; felt good to, for the first time in a long time, lean on a man's shoulders and allow him to carry her-burdens and all. She hadn't felt a man's touch like this since the last time Snow held her in his arms, and that seemed like forever ago. No, she didn't want to forget what it felt like to be sheltered and protected by a man, and have him fulfill her every passion. For a fleeting moment, she bath in Willie's touch-though ordinarily he wasn't fully her type.

Willie pushed V back a little, tilted her head back and laid a soft moist kiss upon her lips. He grasped her tighter, fully expecting her to resist, but to his pleasant surprise, she didn't-at least not right away.

A wave of heat mixed with heavy emotions showered down upon V from her head to her toe. Her breaths quickened as wanton long forgotten breaths of passion eased from her breast and out of her nostrils. Slowly, yet softly she dug her fingernails into Willie's shoulders.

He endured the gentle pain and tried to pull her closer.........and then;

V snapped back, and came to herself as though she couldn't believe herself. How could she let her flesh control her now at such a dire hour of distress- She cannot allow herself to yield to the desires of her weakened flesh; no, she was a new creature now. She was saved and a born again Christian. She cannot yield to a moment of weakness and passionate desires; no, too much was at stake-heaven or hell.

Although her flesh screamed in rebellion, She forced herself to pulled back and tore loose from Willie's arms as he struggled to hold on to her.

"Willie….Willie….Willie…are you….are you crazy. What are you doing.. Please… Please." V labored to say between hard breaths. "The world is coming to an end, and hell has broken out everywhere, and…..and….and your butt is thinking of making out. Are you kidding me; I mean seriously Willie…Really." A few beads of sweat streaked down her brow while her words eased out heavy and laden with forbidden desires.

V rubbed her hands through her hair, and wiped the heated sweat from her forehead, and forced herself to roll her eyes at him. But, even then, she wished that Willie didn't listen to her outward rejection, and hear her inward screams pleading for this moment of passion with him-possibly the last man that she would ever sojourn with on this side of life.

She rubbed her sleeve across her lips, trying hard to pretend not liking what had just happened between them; but, secretly, in the bosom of her heart, she liked what Willie had done. It had been a long time since she really felt a man's touch; had been a long time since she was made to feel like a woman, a sensuous woman. Oh god, she craved that. She didn't know what had become of her beloved Snow, but she had to keep searching until all hope was gone

In her heart, she craved Willie's touch, but she had to pretend for both their sakes; so that they could stay focused on the arduous task at hand-surviving this world wide mayhem.

"V...V, um sorry! Um so sorry! I don't know what came over me! I just don't know. I...I was overwhelmed by your beauty and couldn't help myself. Oh god V please forgive me. I am so sorry, but I'd be lying if I said that it didn't feel good, feel wonderful. I am hurting inside and out so very bad. I just needed a woman's touch; not just any touch, but yours V. I've always been attracted to you." Willie stumbled through his explanation.

"But, you're married Willie." V stumbled to say between short suppressed breaths.

"No, I used to be. You know that my wife is gone, taken with the rest of the vanished people; so I am single and you are single. What is wrong with us marrying each other now and enjoying what little degree of life we have left together?" Willie said, with as much passion as he could muster, while looking to see what V's reaction would be.

"Life has to go on. I don't think that God intended for us to stop living; and whether you believe or not, Snow is gone-at least the Snow we knew."

"Ahhh." V moaned in frustration, knowing that Willie was right, but not wanting to fully accept it.

"I can make you happy if you allow me to. We are already in this together. Why not comfort each other during our quest to survive these times. I need you, and you need me, whether you want to accept it or not." Willie said, pleading.

"I know…I know, but…but.. .but I need a lil time Willie." She eased out; head still resting on the steering wheel.

"But time is not something that we have, and right now, it is not on our side. We must live in each moment, for we don't know what the next one will bring." Willie said softly while reaching over and touching her softly on her shoulder.

"I know, god knows, I know all to well." She said, raising up and wiping a few lonely tear drops from her face. "We need to settle down some place to call home sooner or later. Some place to make our last defense, some place where death will receive us." She reached up and placed her hand upon Willie's hand that was resting gently upon her shoulder.

During V's moment of feminine frailty, Willie eased in to try and kiss her once again'

Just then, amidst Willie's pleading explanation of yielding temptation, three missiles zoomed across the awakening sky headed for some unsuspecting target. Moments later a colony of drones flew over their heads in the same direction the missiles had just gone.

The last of night was quickly easing away, and somebody was about to be bombed to hell and back by China's angry attack.

"Let's get out of here V!" Willie shouted, still looking up at the sky full of drones.

"On it!" V shouted out while popping her seat back up and cranking the mustang.

The tires squealed, as they zoomed down the road in the opposite direction of the missiles and drones. Moments later, they heard loud explosions and watched smoke fill the sky. V kept going as fast as the mustang would take them.

The engine kept roaring and reaching for more roads to conquer. V kept shifting gears and popping the clutch until they were seemingly a safe distance away from the bombing carnage. The war had found its way to them-China was advancing to conquer the West.

The whole world was at war; and with almost two billion people, China had an endless supply of soldiers willing and ready to die for their country. All seemed hopeless; Russia, United States, China, France, United Kingdom, Pakistan, India, Israel, North Korea, and a host of other countries, all had nuclear weapons that could annihilate the whole planet in a moment.

The whole world could be blown to pieces at any time. Life on earth could be completely wiped out. If just one of the Nations launched their nuclear weapons, then the rest will respond in like manner-all will die at once-maybe earth itself would be obliterated, or, at the very least, thrown back into the ice age with very few humans dwelling on earth.

Airplanes rushed across the laden sky. Bombs whistled just before crashing to the already wrath filled earth.

V kept pressing hard on the gas pedal, and the mustang kept reaching for more road. A bomb hit the middle of the road and tore it to pieces, leaving a cradle the size of a car. V swerved hard, trying to avoid the flying shrapnel. The mustang sailed off the road into the air and landed hard into a corn field. V shifted back down to third gear, stomped the gas pedal, the mustang roared like a madden beast, and started zooming through the corn field with the vengeance of a betrayed lover. The loud sound of snapping and popping corn stalks riddled the air like a soldier's machine gun. V shifted another gear-pinning Willie to the seat. He held on for dear life.

"V…V…V, What are you doing. You trying to kill us, ain't you?" Willie yelled out at V, staring wide eyed into the high stalks of corn. "Where are you going? Can you see? I can't see nothing but corn. Oh god, we gone die! We gone die today in this field of corn! The white folks are gone find our black butts with corn shoved up our noses. Help us Jesus. Lord save us!"

"Willie if you don't shut up, I swear to god um a grabbed one of these stalks of corn and shove it down your throat! I swear!" She shouted over at Willie, taking her eyes off the corn and looking angrily over at Willie. "What are we supposed to do? Stop in the middle of this field and let the car get stuck? Huh? What we supposed to do Willie?"

"But I can't see anything." Willie shouted back.

"Me neither, so that makes us even!" She shouted hard over at him while staring straight ahead- trying to see what she could see between the high stalks of corn.

Suddenly, the mustang shot out from the tall corn and up a dirt embankment into the air. Willie hollered. "Oh Lord, this woman trying to drive to heaven! Help us Jesus; help us!"

V braced herself for a hard landing. The mustang hit the road hard, almost rolling over as it zoomed on two wheels for a moment. V down shifted and kept rolling-refusing to stop for nothing and nobody.

"This baby ain't nothing but the truth!" V screamed passionately into the air. "You hear me Willie? This baby is the truth."

"Yea, you gone ride us straight to hell if you ain't careful." Willie started raising his hands in the air and shouting.

"Yea, but what a ride-huh? What a ride bruh."

Soon, the mustang was back on all four tires and dashing down the dirt road. V kept giving it all she had.

"Girl, you are a driving something….You can drive. I don't care what nobody says. You can drive! Why, I'll ride with you anywhere." Willie said excitedly, waving his hands in the air and looking over at V.

V just looked over at him with a big smile spread across her face as the mustang straddled the road and reached for more speed.

Suddenly, without any indication, there appeared to fall from the sky, fifty yards in front of them, a strange looking man riding a strange looking horse.

V slammed on brakes, trying not to run into the horseman; the mustang slid to a stop just a few yards from the horseman; and then, before the bust could settle, two other horsemen hit the ground hard on each side of them- looking just like the horseman in front of them.

"What the…" V started to say.

"Lord Jesus, if we ever did need you, we show need you right now." Willie said with a shaking voice while staring up at the sky. "Those beasts, or whatever they are, look to be nothing but trouble; and Lord you know I don't want no trouble. Save us Lord, save us right now Jesus."

V shifted the mustang to reverse and started to back up, but before she could, a fourth horseman slammed to the ground with the force of a shattering bomb. Now V and

Willie were surrounded by the terrifying horsemen on terrifying looking horses. There was no way of escape. They just sat there for what seemed like forever and stared at the creatures that had them surrounded.

The horsemen had on armory breastplates that burned with a golden glowing fire that didn't consume them. Long straggly blond hair hanged ridged upon their broad shoulders. They just stared, not speaking and unmoving, through the blazing fire at V and Willie, as if waiting for command.

The horses had the head of a ferocious lion with a heavy mane, and long sharp teeth that protruded from their mouths like daggers, and their tales were long with the head of a serpent, with red eyes, that swirled from side to side and hissed behind them.

"Well, what's next?" V questioned to herself, not expecting an answer from Willie.

"Oh, I know what they are going to do. They gone kill us and have us for dinner." Willie said, not taking his eyes off of the four horsemen.

"Willie… Willie, get a hold of yourself. I don't need to hear that kind of talk right now. I am trying to figure out how we gone get out of this mess." She said.

The horse and its rider, in front of them, started to prance and turn around and around as though it wanted to break free of its rider.

The rider pointed his long shining spear at them.

V wanted to reach for her stick shift, and punch the gas-at least try something, but something wouldn't allow her to move, or to say anything further to Willie. She was frozen; Willie was frozen too, staring up at the scary blond haired horsemen.

A burst of aluminous light shot from his spear and landed on the forehead of V and Willie. It knocked them back in their seats, and pinned their heads hard against the seat rest. V wanted to scream, but nothing would come out of her mouth.

"This is the end of us." She thought to herself. "When I need and want him to say something, he sits over there all quiet." She thought of Willie amongst her piercing thoughts.

The light pressed something upon their foreheads and in the palms of their hands. They could feel the impressions.

"Now, you too wear the Lord's seal of protection against the warriors and plagues of the earth. We go now to lead our armies against those of the antichrist and his beast, and against the False prophet, and against soldiers from Southeast Asia-the land that you humans call China. We shall slay a third of all human flesh." He spoke loudly while his lips were hidden amidst the burning golden fire that blazed his breast plate. "The Lord of Lords will return soon; be ready."

With his last words, they and their horses began to ride off into the distance, finally disappearing amongst the raging dust that followed them.

"I don't know whether to be happy or sad," said V.

"Why? Sounds like good news for us to me. I am more than happy. Now we don't have to worry about them locus and that other stuff that the bible says is soon to come."

"Really, Willie you're only thinking about yourself. When are you going to start thinking about others and how you can help them survive?" V snapped.

"Well, I am thinking about us." Willie said sheepishly.

"Awww!" V moaned with frustration, and then shift the gear, punched the gas and headed in the opposite direction that those scary horsemen road in.

CHAPTER TEN

New Life

Revelation 20: 5-6

5. But the rest of the dead lived not again until the thousand years were finished. This is the first resurrection.

6. Blessed and holy is he that has [art in the first resurrection; on such the second death has no power, but they shall be priests of God and of Christ, and shall reign with him a thousand years.

Slowly, struggling to get on his feet and get the weighted heap of fallen debris off of him, and moaning loudly as he pushed his way through, Snow gasped hard, as would be fresh air raced into his mouth and down into his lungs. Staggering, he stood up and stumbled to walk as streaks of pain raced through his legs. He was thirsty, hungry, dirty and beaten by whatever or whoever, but it didn't even matter because now he was still alive; though he couldn't remember anything, he was definitely alive and seemingly well.

"You can't kill me!" He screamed as loud as he could into the empty lowering sky-flaying his arms as he did. "I ain't that easy to kill. You can't kill me!"

Snow kept angrily screaming into the air at everyone, no one, and anyone that could hear him. He rationed that, no doubt, someone had tried to kill him and thought that he was dead; for trouble was his life style-like breathing, it came natural for him.

He stumbled over to an overturned chair, stood it upright and sat down hard. He patted his pockets in search of a cigarette. It seemed that whoever had done this to him had emptied his pockets of everything; only dust and sand filled his pockets. He ran his hands through his dreadlock hair, and was a bit surprised that they didn't cut them off. He was known for his dreads. The strangers on the streets always referred to him as the white boy with the dreads.

He tried hard to think of what had happened to him, but he kept coming up empty-a blank.

"Yea, it's hell isn't it?" A smooth voice eased upon him.

Startled, Snow whirled around to see who it was talking to him; though, the voice sounded familiar, still, he couldn't place it.

"They thought that they had finally got you; had finally silenced the great Snow." Morrow said, stepping even closer to Snow. "Well, so they thought. Fools, never realize that you can't easily kill people of purpose. People of purpose will find a way to walk away and fulfill their destiny; it's in their DNA to achieve what the Father has commissioned them to do. You can't kill a purpose; they refuse to stop dreaming. It is the only thing that has kept you alive all this time."

"Oh, now it's coming back…Morrow, my friend. You look a lil different." Snow stuttered sarcastically as he shook his head from side to side still trying to get the confusion out and remember something. "What happened? What's going on?"

"Yea, I been through a bit of hell too while you were taking your nap. I mean, somebody has to watch the house while you lay sleeping. Those lil want to be thugs are just like flies, they are just a pest to those of us that must be about The Father's business. Their like roaches; always looking for a free meal, but I stopped them."

"What flies? What thugs?" Snow said, amidst swirling thoughts.

"Don't worry; it will all come back to you in a minute. A lot has happened and is happening since you were out. You were probably caught by the debris of the great earth quake; and kept, no doubt, in suspended animation by the Watchers."

"Watchers? What watchers? Who are they?" Snow asked, confused

"If you must know, Angels, whose business is to get into earthlings business; because you all just naturally migrate toward that which is obtuse. They try to keep y'all in the path for which you were created. They also saved many of the humans from the Great earth quake that hit not too long ago."

"Earth quake? What earth quake?" Snow stammered to say.

"Yea; earthquake, locust that torture, bloody water, a world war led by China, and the list goes on and on Bro. You name it and we got it." Morrow said with an air of sarcasms.

Snow ran his hands over his dreads and shook his head, trying to make sense of all of the things that Morrow said were now happening. How could he have possibly been out so long-that's just not possible; he reasoned to himself.

"The rapture; the Great Tribulation period, Oh God! We're in that now?" Snow said, rising to his feet in disbelief. "Where is V? The last I remember is we were trapped at some church…and…and…and there was an explosion or something. I don't remember anything else, but waking up here."

"The Watchers brought you here and placed you out of sight. They're not really up on the frailty of human flesh; which is the reason why they left you in such condition. I know it's a lot to swallow at one time, but it is here and now, and you have got to pull yourself together and deal with where we are-seeing that you play a part in all of this."

"What part? What is all of this? I am just trying to survive; trying to get my life back; my girl back. I didn't ask for any of this." Said Snow, filled with frustration.

"No you didn't, but it kind of started with your father-Reverend Frank senior. Some things are beyond our control; many times it starts with our ancestors." Morrow tried to explain to Snow and comfort him in the same breath.

"I just want my life back with my lady V, and probably a little drama to deal with, but this is ridiculous. We got a world war, locust, blood, moaning and screaming all around me at the same time. What's next?" He said.

"I'd be careful what I asked for if I were you" Morrow said evenly.

"But, you're not me, and I am not you-speaking in all of these riddles and circles that are not making much sense to me."

"Well Snow, let me be the first to tell you. I don't know how, or how deep, but you're in and a part of all of this." Morrow said, easing down, crossing his legs, and sitting on a shattered widow seal.

"What about V? Where is she?" Snow said, gazing deeply into Morrows eyes.

"Don't know; hadn't seen her in a minute. She is probably gone with the rest of them, or dead all together."

"What?" Snow snapped, looking over at Morrow sternly. "Why are you being so callous?"

"Ok...Ok... Ok, that was a little callous of me-my bag; but, for real though, I don't know. I really hadn't seen her, but knowing her; she is a fighter. She probably survived all of this. "

Suddenly, their conversation was interrupted; the sound of loud buzzing off in the distance heading their way. Several explosions sounded off a few miles away as streaks of light flashed through the still sky.

Snow's senses eased back to him, he could hear screaming and hollering not far from them-sounds of pain, fear, and defeat; sounds that he was more than familiar with.

Morrow just stood there erect in anticipation, with his hands folded behind his back, and stared in the direction of the ever increasing buzzing noise. He knew what it was.

A large black cloud of something ferocious was approaching them fast. It was the locust; seemed like millions and millions of them; angry and looking for somebody to torture or kill. The closer they got, the louder the hellacious noise became. It was mingled with more screaming and hollering in the streets.

There were few places to hide from the locusts, and only God's marked children were safe from them. They were simply beast from hell on earth; released to torture and suffer man- the inhabitants on the earth.

They flew in innumerably and surrounded Morrow and Snow. With their face of a man with long blond hair that draped upon their shoulders and a long tail curled over like a scorpion's tail with large pulses of poison dripping from it. They were the size of a large dog-a hideous forsaken kind of creature that even a glance of them filled most men with overwhelming fear. Ready to strike at any moment, they sat and stared hard-mostly at Snow. The creatures kept flying in until the streets and everything, as far as one could see, were covered with these locusts.

"What do we do?" Snow said softly to Morrow, almost whispering, and measuring his every movement. "What can we do?"

"Nothing, absolutely nothing. Just pray that we're not on their menu." Morrow said almost too casually, as though not weighing the danger that they were in.

Snow looked over at him in disbelief-How could Morrow joke in such a time as this? He thought that they were about to die at any given moment. He felt helpless, completely helpless, and that was not a feeling that Snow was accustomed too.

"Gentlemen; gentlemen." A voice spoke softly from a brilliantly glowing man as he meticulously stepped out of the blackness of the locust.

It was Apollyon; the chief Angel of the bottomless pit who was the leader of these horrific torturous locusts. He was a little over seven feet tall and clad with a tailored white three piece suit that looked like it was sculptured just for him. His long illuminating white hair with hinted locks of curls rested easily just beyond his broad shoulders; it was obvious to see that hidden under that brilliant fabric was a sculptured body with broad shoulders and a trimmed waist line connected to thighs that were chiseled like trunks of trees. His deep set eyes, nestled amongst pronounced cheek bones, sparkled and beamed as he gazed upon Snow and Morrow.

"Ahhhh… The refined locust prince, Apollyon, from the bottomless pit. my brother, to what do I owe this pleasure? " Morrow mused at the regal angel.

"I'd watch my tone if I were you." Apollyon evenly snapped at Morrow. "Been awhile since I have seen any action, and though I might be a little battle rusty, non-the-less, I am most able to vanquish most of my enemies. Of course, prince Morrow, you already know that."

"Prince?" Snow whispered softly, gazing over at Morrow. "Something I should know here? When did you become a prince Morrow?"

"Oh, you didn't know? Morrow is an angel- an angel just like me. Word is, he lost his power fooling with puny humans like you." Apollyon continued. "And, he has lots and lots of enemies; so, Mr. Snow, that is what you call yourself isn't it? Now you know."

"Yea, I kind of figured as much, but what I got to do with yall's squabble? Just tell your little hungry creatures to stand down and let me be on my way, and y'all just catch up in this reunion."

"You don't, and yet you do." Apollyon hissed. "And, Morrow and I have no, how you say.....errr...squabble. We're just crossing paths amidst you-a puny powerless, insignificant mortal. Me and my locusts have been given the wonderful pleasure to torment you insolent ungrateful creatures-made from the dirt of the earth."

"Just crossing paths. Yea right. I doubt that?" Snow said sarcastically.

"I would chat a little longer and catch up Morrow, but you know, business is business, and as I said, it's been a minute," said Apollyon.

Before either of them could respond, Apollyon turned and eased gracefully back from where he came, into the blackness of the hissing locust creatures; and then, in the haze of a loud buzzing, all consuming, blacken cloud, the locust and Apollyon sped off into the sky.

God awful screaming invaded the air as the locusts perused through the streets. They bit and stung everybody that crossed their path.

Men and women heads and bodies were swollen all over; blood rushed from their wounds and seeped to the parched thirsty ground. The more they screamed the more excited the locusts became. They attacked houses and stores and every crack and craves that they could find; bursting out windows and invading by the thousands. It was their jobs to torture- God the Father had given them the right to. They could not be killed, stopped, or even slowed down. They flew all together searching for their next terrified victim.

But, men and women still would not accept Jesus, and repent from the wickedness. The more that they were tortured, the more that they hated God, and was drawn to this new world leader, Abu Nebuchez.

A lone man of God, stood on the corner and preached to the people amidst the swarming locusts dishing out much suffering and disdain. The locusts continued their quest as though he wasn't even there; they knew who belonged to God and who didn't.

"Repent and accept The Lord Jesus as your savior, and you can be spared from the torment of these locusts sent by God to torment the wicked for their evil ways. Jesus is your only hope! You cannot escape nor hide from this time of Judgement commissioned by The Father of all things; how be it, even time obeys his voice. Accept His Son, Jesus, before it is too late. He will sooth your tormented body and soul. The Holy word says that if you confess your sins and accept Jesus as your savior, you shall be saved; but, if not, the cost of sin is eternal suffering and death." This preacher kept on preaching amidst the mayhem of screaming and suffering. He hoped and prayed, in his heart, that someone would come and accept the welcome of The Father, but none did.

One of the tortured victims, pulled out his long knife and lunged it deep into his own neck, hoping to sever his artery and die; he did, and blood came gushing out, but he remained alive and felt the anguish painful attack of the locust while they bathed in his rich oxygenated red blood.

Many of the afflicted ran to the top of buildings, trying to escape with the locusts clinging to them and gnawing on their flesh. They leaped and splattered onto the hard sidewalk like chunks of ice from a hail storm, but to no avail, they were still alive; broken bones-arms, necks, backs, legs, but still alive, and tortured by the locust.

The preacher kept on screaming amidst the pandemonium, " Repent...Repent.....Repent. Please repent, for the Father still loves you. There be but one way to escape this torment, for even death refuses to ease your suffering. Accept Jesus right now. You still have time."

CHAPTER ELEVEN

time to choose sides

Revelation 13: 13-17

13. And he does great wonders, so that he makes fire come down from heaven on the earth in the sight of men,

14. And deceives them that dwell on the earth by the means of those miracles which he had power to do in the sight of the beast: saying to them that dwell on the earth, that they should make an image to the beast, which had the wound by a sword, and did live.

15. And he had power to give life unto the image of the beast, that the image of the beast should both speak, and cause that as many as would not worship[the image of the beast should be killed.

16. And he caused all, both small and great, rich and moor, free and bond, to receive a mark in their right hand, or in their foreheads:

17. And that no man might buy or sell, save he that had the mark, or the name of the beast, or the number of his name.

Abu Nebuchez gathered all of his computer and IT experts together-the best in the entire world. He had a major project for them that would effect and control the whole world-every man and woman.

They all sat amazed in what looked like a large university lecture room. They waited, bathed in excitement, for Abu Nebuchez to come and address them. They didn't know what to expect, but they knew that it had to be something big and important.

Suddenly, the lights slowly dimmed, and the stage illuminated brightly as Abu Neuchez crossed the platform, escorted by Eskander-his personal assistant, General Amad-chief of the global military, and a Cardinal Bishop clad in his full cardinal dress with a sheepish smile plastered upon his face as he faintly nodded his head to the audience. The audience of IT experts and AI (artificial

Intelligence) experts erupted in a standing ovation amidst shouts and applauds.

"Please, please, please; thank you, thank you; sit down, take your seats. I assembled you all here because you are the best and the brightest in the world at your crafts, and it is going to take all of us working together to accomplish the task I have envisioned. We have already established the first part-a one world religion-we all shall worship one god, the same god, and every other religion around the globe shall be outlawed. Anybody that worships any other god, shall be executed. I've personally appoint Cardinal Bishop Francesco Russo to head our church. Now, you say what does that have to do with you?" Abu Nebuchez paused and slowly ran his right hand, very gracefully, through his crop top haircut. With a beaming consuming smile plastered upon his lips, he stood erect with his olive skin glowing amidst the lights. "Well, ladies and gentlemen, what I need from you is two things: build me a mega computer that will combined all the computers around the globe, and build me an android in my image with artificial intelligence like non other; that can speak and reason of its own self. He will look like me; think like me, and have my personality. I shall be the only one that will know the difference between my android and me."

"The AI will be connected to the main global commuter that runs everything?" One of the IT experts asked.

"Yes, of course. We will call him the beast-for he will control every part of our daily lives around the whole globe. We will no longer operate with paper money or credit cards either. We shall put a chip upon every man and woman on earth. They will handle all of their business from that chip that will be slightly under their skin on their forehead. And, we shall be able to locate them anywhere at anytime around the globe."

A soft rumble eased through the crowd. They were overtaken by Abu Nebuchez speech to them.

"With all due respect Mr. President, that can't be done!" One of them shouted out. "It would take forever to do that; if such a thing is even possible."

"Bring him up here." President Abu Nebuchez said to the soldiers standing around the walls. "I want to personally show him that it can be done. I must show all of you that it can be done."

They all looked bewildered, wondering just what the president was about to show them; some new technology perhaps.

The soldiers escorted the young scientist to the stage and placed him beside President Abu Nebuchez.

"So you think that it can't be done-huh?" President Nebuchez said, staring sternly into the young man's eyes.

"No, it can't." He replied uneasily, and then looked off into the crowd for some of his constituents approval and agreement.

BANG!!! A loud thunder pierced the air and echoed through the room while some in the crowd screamed out in horror and disbelief.

President Abu Nebuchez had taken one of the soldier's pistols, put it to the young man's temple and pulled the trigger. His brains blew out the other side of his head and splattered onto the wall and curtains adjacent to them. A gaping hole, with brain matter hanging from it, seeped blood onto the mahogany brown hard wood floor. Rich red blood slowly puddled under his head as his eyes stared aimlessly up at the vaulting ceiling.

"Anybody else doesn't believe that it can be done?" President Nebuchez shouted while waving the gun casually across the crowded room as he spoke. "Now is the time to speak up. We only have room for people that believe, everybody else will be shot. You're either in or you're out. All that is in will be well accommodated; I promise you. The only way that you can't do it is you are no longer breathing-like this fellow."

Cardinal Bishop Francesco Russo nervously and uneasily stepped to the murdered young man's body-still staring aimlessly at the ceiling, and began to perform the last rights over him.

"Stop!" President Abu Nebuchez shouted at the Cardinal. "You only do last rights over those that I instruct you to; is that clear Cardinal Russo?"

"Yes, yes, as you wish Mr. President." Cardinal Bishop Francesco Russo said very softly-almost whispering, clearly shaken by the president's appalling actions. He stepped back in his place.

Eskander was more than startled; he had never seen this side of President Abu Nebuchez before, but he had to quickly pull himself together or else he would be next; he thought to himself.

"Damned infidel scoundrel, how dare he tell the president what can't be done." General Amad said, un-holstering his own 45 from his side, and then shot twice into the chest of the already dead man.

The ladies in the crowd screamed again. They could not believe what they were witnessing. Many were openly sobbing.

President Abu Nebuchez looked over at General Amad and nodded his head approvingly, then handed the soldier's gun back over to him. He moved over to the other side of the stage, trying to get away from the bleeding corpse. Eskander, General Amad, and Cardinal Bishop Francesco Russo followed in sync.

"Now, as I was saying, before that idiot so rudely interrupted me. I need a master computer that will connect everybody around the globe, and issue everybody a number upon the chip in their foreheads; a number that can be tracked anywhere in the world. And, let's get rid of paper money period. All of their credit worthiness will be on the chip planted in their foreheads. And, I need an android with supreme artificial intelligence that looks identical to me that can think and reason as I do. And, Cardinal Bishop Francesco Russo will give the world my religion and have every man and woman worshipping me. I am their god. I need this done yesterday, for time is not on our side." President Abu Nebuchez spoke firmly and evenly as he gestured intently with his hands, and then, He leaned over and whispered softly into General Amad's ear.

The General motioned to three of his armed soldiers, carrying machine guns, to come up on the stage. When they came up, he whispered into their ears; they nodded their heads yes, and then stepped to the edge of the stage with their weapons pointing at the audience.

"I feel that some of you are not getting what I am saying, and don't realize the urgency of this matter, so I need to impress upon you that I mean business, and failure is not an option." President Abu Nebuchez said with a hint of a frown on his face. He then raised his right hand high into the air, and then dropped it to his side. When his palm touched his thigh, the soldier's machine guns roared and sprayed everybody in the front row of seats-about fifty scientist and computer scholars.

The rest of the audience erupted in screams and cries, but they didn't leave their seats, for they knew better-they would be next.

The auditorium filled with smoke and the smell of gunpowder. Men and women were sobbing at the pointless deaths.

"I hope that I have made myself clear here today. No one is indispensable amongst you. Follow orders and you live; you don't, you die. Everybody understand me?" He asked.

No one said anything; only sobbing filled the air. He raised his hand high into the air again.

"No…No…Wait, stop, we understand Mr. President. We understand!" One of the scientists yelled out. "We will get it done. You will have your Beast computer, your android, and chips ready to implant in every forehead in the world, and we will accept you as our God; just please don't slay any more of us. We are just scientist and computer geeks that love our jobs, and you, our president. We will make it happen."

"What is your name?" President Abu Nebuchez said, looking down at the young scientist, now with a welcoming smile on his face as though none of his horrific actions had occurred.

"My name is Jeremiah, Jeremiah Stien sir."

"Well Mr. Stein, are you a doctor or a computer geek?" Asked President Abu Nebuchez with a hint of humor.

"I am both Mr. President. I am a computer science engineer. I love building computers and its software."

"Then, I shall put you in charge of this project. You will report directly to me, and you shall move into my mansion immediately. I suggest that you assemble the best of the best and work around the clock. Are we clear Doctor Jeremiah Stien?"

"Yes sir Mr. President. I shall get on it right away, and move into your premises imminently."

"You all have a wonderful rest of your day." President Nebuchez said to the audience as he waved at them and strutted briskly from the stage with Eskander, General Amad, and Cardinal Bishop Francesco Russo following closely behind him.

It was obvious that they all were still a little uneasy with this new side of President Nebuchez; a side that they had never seen before.

CHAPTER TWELVE

A New World to embrace

Revelation 12: 7-8

7, And there was war in heaven: Michael and his angels fought against the devil; and the devil fought with his angels,

8. and prevailed not; neither was their pace found any more in heaven.

Revelation 13: 15-17

15. And he had power to give life unto the image of the beast, that the image of the beast should both speak, and cause that as many as would not worship the image of the beast should be killed.

16. And he caused all, both small and great, rich and poor, free and bond, to receive a mark in their right hand, or in their forehead.

17. And that no man might buy or sell, save he that had the mark, or the name of the beast, or the number of his mane.

China, with its 200,000,000 army was now joined by a hungry, for power, North Korea, Russia, Cuba, Vietnam, and many other nations, now waged war with Abu Nebuchez in an attempt to rule the entire world. Their plan was a one world government under a new world order —adjacent to a communistic system.

Right then, all land, all businesses, and all the people were owned by the government-Abu Nebuchez. He owned everybody and everything, but the other nations had come together to outs Abu Nebuchez.

President Abu Nebuchez closed all the prisons everywhere around the world, and turned them into lavish hotels where the rich and those that had served him well could go and be served and spoiled by President Abu Nebuchez servants. There weren't any reminders of the building having used to be a prisons filled with murderous inmates;

inmates that the government had clothed, housed, and fed for many years, particularly those that were on death row.

President Abu Nebuchez said that prisons served no purpose. He set up courts all over the world, and everyone was judged-either innocent or guilty- No prison time; the innocent was set free, and the guilty was executed that same day by a firing squad; So, needless to say, crime around the world dropped to almost zero; because, for the minutest offence against the law, one was immediately executed, with no appeals allowed-if you break the law, you die.

President Abu Nebuchez made it the law that no one lived past the age of fifty-nine; everyone was euthanized on the sixth month of their fifty-ninth birthday. They were given a lethal injection of pentobarbital, midazolam, or fentanyl.

The President felt that the elderly had served their purpose and was now an unwarranted expense to the country-youth was a luxury, and nobody ever boasted of their age or celebrated birthdays-longevity of age had become a curse. He closed all nursing homes and senior care facilities. President Nebuchez said that there was no need for them, seeing that there weren't going to be any seniors.

At fifty-nine years old, the government shuts off the identification mark on everybody so that they could no longer buy, sell, or trade in society, and if, at the appointed time, they didn't turn themselves in to be euthanized, then, the government would hunt them down and execute them on sight; so all that were fifty-nine and above were forced to become rebels and enemies of the state. They were in hiding and on the run.

"I can't go any further; um tired, um hungry, and my bones just hurt," said Pocket. "I ain't had a good night's sleep in I don't know when. We on the run like common criminals and outlaws just because we're over fifty-nine years old. Who would have figured that it would be against the law to get old?"

"And don't forget, ain't no children on earth either-no children and no old folks. President Nebuchez done lost his rabbit mind." Pa Frank said, scratching his head and then running his hands down through his scraggly gray beard.

"Amen to that." Pocket said, still looking out through the bushes without ever turning around.

"Well, I guess that fool forgot he gone get old one day too." Pa Frank eased out, staring through the tall bushes. "What he gone do then? I bet he will extent the age then."

"No, he knows that time will wrap up long before he can get old. The Lord will return soon, and he knows it. He just trying to kill all the seasoned saints that have wisdom and strength enough to stand, fight, and keep on praying." Mr. Archie said, trying to calm their fears. "Remember, the Bible says that if these days of tribulation were not shortened, nobody would be saved."

"Well, we still alive ain't we." Pocket said softly. "If you can call this living-hiding in bushes and running from the government that wants to kill you just because God has blessed you with long life, and sixty ain't even old. man, I got socks older than that."

"Shoot, you call this living." Mr. Pocket whipped, almost amidst anger.

"Well, if you tired of living like this and you are ready to die, you know what to do; just get out of these bushes and walk casually in the streets and one of them government workers will help you stop breathing." Pa Frank eased out as he peeped out through the bushes at the adjacent road. "Life is always filled with choices."

"What choices? They didn't give us a choice. They just said that everybody fifty-nine and up will be killed. What is the world with no old folk and no children? I didn't choose this. No, cause I'd choose to still be at Pa Franks store playing checkers out front and gazing at the pretty ladies coming through the front door.

"Yes you did. You chose to stay here when all the other saved folk and children were raptured to heaven." Pa Frank said, still looking out the bushes and onto the empty road.

"Hush, I hear something." Mr. Archie said, motioning with his hands for them to get lower to the ground.

Several men in green soldier fatigues perused the area coming towards them.

"Well gents, I guess this is it. They are sure to find us. Y'all keep low and don't move. I am going to buy you some time; good luck and I'll see you on the other side. I'll be eating steak with the angels after while. I love you guys. Remember, stay on the ground and don't move." Mr. Pocket said as he dashed as fast as he could out of the brushes and away from the soldiers coming their way. He prayed to himself that they wouldn't shoot him too fast before he could put some distance between them and his friends- Mr. Archie and Pa Frank.

"Wait, wait, Pocket." Before Archie could finish his sentence, Pocket was off and running as fast as he could away from the soldiers to draw them away from Mr. Archie and Pa Frank.

"Look at this fool. Knows he old and can't run too fast. Lord, please save Pocket and forgive him for his foolish thoughts." Before Archie could finish his words, the men in fatigues were chasing after Pocket.

Mr. Archie and Pa Frank just stared out through the stickled drenched bushes as they watched the men in green fatigues run Pocket down in no time. And though he had only run a very short distance, Mr Pocket stumble and slammed onto the ground amidst riddled pain streaking across his chest. He lay there breathing hard and heavy as the men approached him.

"Well, I guess…..I guess… this is it." He labored to say, and shut his eyes as tight as he could; expecting to be shot at any second.

"Hey, old G, what you doing man? You trying to give yourself a heart attack?" One of the men said as he and one of his comrades reached down and lifted Mr. Pocket off the ground and out of the bushes.

Mr. Pocket looked at them confused and frightened.

They began to pull the bandanas off their faces. Mr. Pocket saw the mark of the Lord on their foreheads. He started crying with tears of joy-still laboring to breath.

"Yea, we're like you; we refuse to bow down to that antichrist Nebuchez. We'll fight until the end because in the end, we win." One of them said, raising his fist in victory.

"Yea, we win, and we gone give them hell until the Lord returns." Another of them sang out amidst the cheers of the others.

Pa Frank and Mr Archie just laid on the ground and peeped out through the bushes and wondered nervously what was going on with Mr. Pocket.

"My friends are over there tucked in those bushes." Mr. Pocket pointed where Archie and Pa Frank was.

They turned and looked in the direction that Mr. Pocket pointed.

"Well, they looking over here; I guess Pocket spilled the beans on us," said Archie, trying to duck down further in the bush.

"Gosh, I knew that joker wouldn't last long; told on us in a heartbeat." Pa Frank said slightly angered. "But, I guess you can't blame him, but I thought that he would last at least through a few slaps"

"Probably harder than you think being slapped around by a bunch of thugs. I wouldn't want to be in his shoes; and I'd probably tell on y'all too-in a heart be, cause I know that is exactly what you would do." Mr. Archie said still staring over at the men and Pocket.

"Better decide now because here they come marching our way." Pa Frank uttered.

Mr. Pocket and the men walked over to where they were, and surrounded them.

"Come on out guys. Don't be afraid. We're on your side. We're running just like you." The men shouted out at them. "You don't believe us, just ask your friend."

"No, they got me brained washed; so um saying anything." Mr. Pocket joked, snickering a little while thinking of how funny his friends were trying to hide in plain sight.

"Dang gone it, Pocket you play too much and at the wrong time." Mr. Archie complained amidst frustration mingled with fear.

Pa Frank and Mr. Archie slowly and fearfully stood up.

Just then, a car streaked to a hollering halt on the road behind them. Some fell to the ground and readied themselves to fight, while others were too filled with fear to even move to cover themselves. Like a Deer, stuck in the view of headlights, They couldn't move.

It was a candy apple red mustang with the top rolled back, purring in the middle of the deserted road. V, stood up in her seat, with her dark shades plastered over her eyes, and stared sternly over at them with her two 9 millimeters strapped and hanging loosely on her hips.

Willie sat quietly slouched in the passenger seat and braced himself for an obvious attack.

"Must you always make such an entry." Willie said nervously, never taking his eyes off of the folks in the adjacent woods. "You gone get us killed yet; you watch what I tell you; always got to be Wonder Woman, or Super Woman, or any one of those crazy hero women that have too much estrogen in their blood. My monkey butt got to fight just because I am in the car with you." He reached down and nervously laid his 9 in his lap.

"Oh, I knew that they were on our side." V said, sitting down and then stepping out of the car.

"Yea, right, how'd you know Wonder Woman?" He whipped back at her, now with a sigh of relief. "But, you already know that I had your back; right? Come hell or high water, we roll together."

"Cause they are hiding in the bushes. Nebuchez men don't hide in the bushes-they don't have to. It is simple deduction Willie, simple deduction.....Stay with me now; stay with me."

They began to walk towards their new would- be militants, but just then, pandemonium burst forth from the sky like a tornado from a raging storm. Flaming meteors rained from the sky as though God himself had flung them from heaven.

They hit the ground violently and slang molten fire everywhere-far and near. Everything was burning as for as the eye could see-even the ground itself; an endless raging inferno with an appetite to consume anything and everything in its path.

Willie started running back to the car and slid under it, hoping to protect himself from the raining fires from heaven. V ran close behind him, holding her hands over her head. She slid under the mustang alone side Willie.

Fire was everywhere and thick black smoke filled the air- The flaming meteors kelp on falling, and falling. A bombing sound echoed through the air as the meteors endlessly pounded the ground and shot dust and pebbles of rock back into the air.

"Well, look like we're about to be burned alive!" Willie shouted over at V. "At least we won't have to burn twice- here and in hell. Looks like we gone get to heaven sooner than we had planned."

The mustang's gas tank exploded into a million pieces, but yet it didn't touch V and Willie.

They secretly thought to themselves that they were done; no way out, and V was sure that the people that they saw in the bushes were dead-burned alive. She could hear the screams of pain and torment all around her.

The meteors were mixed with fire and blood; blood ran profusely everywhere and puddled in the crevices, pot holes, and ditches along the road. Everything that wasn't burning was blood red. Some of the fires, the splattered blood had put out, and there stood clotted blood hanging from blackened chard trees.

They heard a multitude of voices, not wailing voices or voices filled with pain; no, they seem to be voices of praise and worship. V thought that she was hallucinating-no way anybody having church in this hell of a situation.

Thunder rumbled and roared loudly while bolts of lightning streaked across the sky, some streaking down to the ground and electrifying anything in its path. It struck boulders and shattered them in pieces, and struck trees, large trees, and split them in half.

Though he had been scared many a times, Willie had never been this scared before in his life; he trembled all over in fear. He wanted to stop shaking and try and comfort V for the last time, but he couldn't-he just couldn't. He was simply too scared-swallowed up by his own fear.

The mustang was on fire, and Willie felt that he too was about to burn. The heat intensified. He grabbed V and held her close to him; she just kept her face in her hands, trying desperately not to succumb to this horrible fate, but what could she do? What could she do? She hated feeling helpless. All of her life, she had to fend for herself, and she usually succeeded, but this was out of her control; she was helpless.

The intense heat from the burning Mustang began to become unbearable. Then suddenly, the raging fire stopped and a cool simmering breeze eased upon them. The mustang and everything around them just ceased to burn-not even simmering smoke lingered, but it still looked like a once fiery battlefield.

V could see from under the car footsteps walking easily towards them. She pushed Willie hard upon his shoulder, trying to get him to look up and see what she saw.

Willie's head was buried in his hands. He waited for death to come, and hoped and prayed that it would be quick and painless; he never could stand a lot of pain-even as a kid.

She hunched Willie again-harder this time.

"Look!" She managed to say; praying that it wasn't one of President Abu Nebuchez people.

"Are we dead yet? Lord help us!" Willie shouted.

"No, we ain't dead." V shouted over at him. "Must you always be so scared and full of drama? My God! Look." V pointed at the sneakers coming towards them.

"Is it an angel?" V asked filled with hope.

"I don't know, but I ain't never seen no angel wearing Converse sneakers." Willie said.

"Yea, you right; an angel would be wearing Air Jordan." A man's sonorous voice eased out, almost politely.

The sneakers stopped right in front of them. They didn't know what to think or what to believe. Had some supernatural being wearing tennis shoes come to save them? V asked herself.

"This can't be good." Willie moaned, trembling. "Lord help us!"

"Will you settle for me instead?" Morrow asked, bending over and peering at them under the car with a big smile plastered on his face. "Boy, you guys sure know how to find trouble. I bet y'all work your guardian angel to death.'

"Yea, we keep him pretty busy now- a- days." Willie said crawling out from under the torched smoking Mustang while turning back to help V out from under there too.

They stood up and looked at the sky all around them. Everything still burned. People were running amongst the blazing forest that was now an all- consuming inferno, and blazing molten meteors still rained from the smoke filled grey ski.

It seemed like they were shielded by some kind of huge strange bubble that glistened strangely as it kept all the fire and turmoil outside of them-even though, it was evident that the fires had ravished and almost burned up the inside of the protective bubble. It was as though someone or something had come and doused the fire out to save them, but outside, it still raged, and people were still tormented. They were on fire and burning, but none died-they just kept on burning and screaming in pain.

"Morrow! My man! Boy am I glad to see you!" Willie shouted flaying his arms around Morrow's shoulders. "I don't know how you do these things, but you are always somehow saying our butts from something or somebody. Man, you rock. And, I don't want to know what you are, or what you ain't, just save us when we need you-Ok." Willie ranted on and on. As usual,

V just stared at him and rolled her eyes up to the sky, and then she looked outside, beyond the glistening bubble where the fires still raged and the meteors continued crashing to the earth drenched in blood. The people still wailed in anguish pain and suffering.

Tears rolled down her face and lapped under her chin. She wished that she could do something to save all of them, but then, she realized that she couldn't even save herself.

Morrow looked over at her, while Willie stood silent for a minute. He could feel V's pain and sorrow for the burning people. Many of them ran up to the bubble and beat upon it, pleading for them to let them in.

V looked at Morrow questioningly as a few more tears leaped down her face. She hated to cry. Her mama always taught her that tears was a sign of weakness, so don't let nobody see you cry-nobody; but this time she couldn't help it. The tears just kept on coming like they had a mind of their own.

"There is nothing I can do V; even if I wanted to. I am but a servant of the Most High God, creator of Heaven and earth. They chose their fate when they accepted the mark of Nebuchez. He is the Antichrist. They forfeited their souls to eternal damnation." He turned and looked at the young lady, burning and pounding her fist upon the bubble until blood mixed with fire dripped from them and streaked down the side of the bubble.

Willie came up and hugged both of them, and he too began to weep, but his tears were tears of thankfulness because it could have very well been him, and would have been him, a hypocritical pastor that preached every Sunday but lived an ungodly life. He had changed and asked God for forgiveness after he found that his wife and little girl were raptured to heaven without him.

"What are we going to do? We can't stay here forever." V managed to say. "And we can't go out there."

"Yea, what we gone do Morrow? You got any more tricks up your sleeves? We sure could use one right about now." Willie mustered to say, looking over Morrow's shoulders at the pain and suffering of the burning people.

"It is so hard to get you all to keep the faith and walk by faith, believing that the Father will take care of you. Gosh." Morrow said, obviously irritated.

The both of them just dropped their heads in sync, knowing full-well that Morrow was right.

"Ok, I am about to open you a way out." Morrow said, and then raised his hands high into the air; suddenly the blood drenched meteors, the fire, and the burning suffering people, like an obedient storm, started moving southward, away from the bubble, and then the bubble that had saved them, just disappeared.

Willie looked down that long chard road, and then looked over at V. They had no place to go and no direction in mind, and if they did, they had no way to get there.

"And how are we going to get where ever it is that we're supposed to be going? Morrow, we can't just walk you know, because if we do, we're already doomed." V said; like most humans, they had already forgotten that God had just saved them from a burning blood drenched, fiery meteorite storm.

"Yea, doomed; I think" Willie said. "But you know that I am still on your side Bro." Willie uttered, hitting his chest with his fist.

Morrow pointed sternly over their shoulders.

The two of them whirled around to see what it was that Morrow was pointing at. V screamed. Filled with joy and excitement, she couldn't believe her eyes. She covered her mouth with both her hands, trying to contain the over whelming joy she felt.

"All snap; now that's what um talking bout. " Willie said, grabbing V and swirling her around in joy. "See there; Bro. You a boss. You are a boss; that's all I got to say. You a boss Bro."

Morrow just smile sheepishly and shook his head at how easily they could turn from sadness to joy over such insignificant things.

V and Willie still just stood there in amazement, and then in unison, they ran over to Morrow and hugged him tightly. She started to cry tears of joy."

"Now you done done something making lady of steal cry. I told you, you a boss. Man, you a boss." Willie just kept on saying it.

She just could not believe her eyes. She had to be dreaming, she thought to herself.

"Yea, I am dreaming. That's it, um dreaming, and in a minute I am going to wake up. Come on pinch me Willie." She said, swirling and looking at Willie.

"Huh?"

"Pinch me. If um dreaming, I'll wake up..Pinch me!" She shouted again at Willie.

He pinched her hard on her shoulder.

She jumped and grabbed her shoulder, and hit Willie on the chest.

"Well, you told me to pinch you hard." Willie said, smiling broadly like he enjoyed pinching her.

"Can we please stay focused here?" Morrow said, pointing again a few feet from them.

There, on the other side of the road, was parked the candy apple red mustang looking as new as it ever was-shining and glistening like it had never been burned or blown up. Its engine purred softly as if it was ready to go.

"But, I saw it blow up and burn," said V.

"Yea, and we were under it." Willie agreed.

"This can't be the same car. It just can't." She said.

"Oh but it is." Morrow said as he strode towards the mustang. "It's the same car; only better."

"But, what about our stuff?" Willie asked in amazement.

"It's all in there."

V ran up to the mustang and slid her hands down the side and over the door mirrors. She just couldn't believe it. She opened the door and slid onto the seat and ran her hands smoothly around the steering wheel, then over the shifter as though she was still trying to convince herself that it is truly real.

Willie got in on the other side, and slid back and forth on the seat like a little kid at Christmas. He just grinned, and then he reached under the front seat where he usually kept his 9 millimeter stored out of sight, but easy to get to. It was there-locked and loaded and ready to spit at a moment's notice.

The other people came out from behind the chard woods and strode up to the car.

"But, I thought that you all were burned in the fire. I didn't see y'all in the bubble." V said looking a little more than surprised, but happy that they too had survived.

"Yea, we were just scared to move; didn't know what to do, but look at how God saves…Want He do it? This just renews my faith and reinvigorates me to fight this heathen President Abu Nebuchez. He kept us then, and He'll keep us again when we need Him, but we must do our parts and fight the good fight of faith, and spread the Word to others who has not received the mark of the antichrist on their foreheads." One of them spoke sternly.

"Well, I am so happy that you all also survived; well. God also saved you too. I wished that we had room enough for all of you, but."

"No...No...No, don't worry about us. We'll walk where the Lord leads us, and if we need some type of transportation, well, The Lord will provide us while we journey on our way to do Him service."

"Now, y'all must get going because I must be going to help other Believers in distress. Now go," said Morrow as he tapped the hood of the candy apple red mustang.

V pushed in the clutch, shift into first gear, raised the engine and it roared like a young male lion. She popped the clutch and the mustang zipped off down the road. She and Willie raised their hands high in the air and waved goodbye to Morrow and the others

They disappeared beyond the hills headed somewhere, anywhere, and even nowhere, but they were off.

CHAPTER THIRTEEN

The two Beast –out of the earth and out of the sea

Revelation 13: 1-2

1. And I stood upon the sand of the sea, and saw a beast rise up out of the sea, having seven heads and ten horns, and upon his horns ten crowns, and upon his heads the name of blasphemy.

2. And the beast which I saw was like unto a leopard, and his feet were as the feet of a bear, and his mouth, as the mouth of a lion. And the dragon gave him his power and his seat, and great authority.

Revelation 13: 11-12

1. And behold another beast coming up out of the earth; and he had two horns like a lamb, and he spoke as a dragon.

2. And he exercised all the power of the first beast before him, and cause the earth and them which dwell therein to worship the first beast, whose deadly wound was healed.

President Abu Nebuchez sat in his lavishly adorned office, seventy-five by one hundred square feet, with ornaments and art from all over the world gracing his walls. Every piece of furniture was ivory white and most pieces were made of ivory straight from Africa. Mahogany furniture, placed strategically around the room, screamed loudly of his regal taste. An oversized oil painting of himself hanged prominently on the wall off to itself, capturing the power and grandeur for which he so hungered for.

He stared out of his bay window, pondering deeply in thought of what was his next move to captivate the world and bring it completely under his subjection-though he knew that he could not possibly win and defeat the undefeatable God; the very one that created him and everything that is, and was, and shall come to be. His thoughts perused the unanswerable question of what would God possibly send their way next. He already knew what was written in the Bible, but he had come to see that some things came that was not outlined in the Revelation.

Suddenly, interrupting his dismal thoughts, a knock echoed from his mahogany double doors and pierced the silence in the room of opulence.

He didn't say anything; he just stared at the door as if he wished to be someplace else.

The knock rang out again, only this time mingled with a little more urgency.

"Yes." President Abu Nebuchezz sang out.

"It is I sire, Eskandor accompanied by General Amad and Bishop Francesco Russo."

"Enter." The President said softly, tossing his hair and leaning back in his swivel chair."

Eskandor, General Amad, and Bishop Francesco walked briskly into the room and stood in front of the President's long mahogany desk.

"Yes, what is it gentlemen?"

"Well, I made sure that your calendar was clear today." Eskandor said, sliding a few papers onto the President's desk for him to look over. "I have a presentation for you to see from that computer geek that you put over building the android you want-Dr. Adof." Eskandor said, looking onto the papers left in his hand to remember the programmer's name. "We checked it out and we think it is what you wanted."

"Yea, I am empressed," said General Amad, flavored with a strong Spanish accent.

"Yea, me too." Bishop Francesco chimed in while shuffling from side to side uncomfortably, trying to hide his nervousness. Ever after Abu Nebuchezz had murdered all of those innocent computer people in the auditorium, he greatly feared him, and felt that he would slay any and all to get what he wanted. Bishop Francesco felt like his days were numbered. He had sold his sold to follow this egotistical, narcissistic, power hungry man, but there was no turning back. He knew that soon hell would become his new home.

"What?" The President said anxiously. "What is it Eskandor?"

Eskandor clapped his hands as he looked towards the door; in walked Doctor Adof, with several assistants, pushing a long boarded box on a trolley.

"What's this?" Nebuchezz said, now rising to his feet

Drops of sweat started easing down Cardinal Bishop Francesco Russo brow. He didn't know what to expect from the president, but he was persuaded to attend this meeting by Eskandor and General Amad. When the world was normal, and he had a normal parish of members, he would oftentimes preach to his members that, "it's bad to live in hell, and then die and go to hell." He was now living those sentiments; for if the Bible was true, and he had received the mark in his skin, he knew that there was no way for him to escape eternal damnation. He hoped that they had gotten the Bible's interpretation wrong.

"Mr. President," said Doctor Adolf, while dismantling the package that stood before them. "I present to you Mr. President-Your replica."

There stood in front of them a computerized man-a robot that looked just like President Abu Nebuchezz.

One of Doctor Adolf's assistants pushed a remote button, and the android came to life and stared directly at the president.

"What the." Abu Nebuchezz started to say.

"You told us to build something that looked just like you; well, here it is," explained Doctor Adolf.

The android looked exactly like the president. Its voiced sounded like the president, and its mannerism was that of the president.

"Mr. President, the only one that will know that it is not you, is you. He is you. He sweats, get angry, laughs, and can perform all task just like you."

"Only better because it's a machine." One of Doctor Adolf's assistant said with a slight grin plaster on his lips.

In an instant, President Abu Nebuchezz casually reached into his desk drawer and pulled out a 38 pistol revolver, pointed it at the assistant's head and pulled the trigger; blood and brain matter flung violently across the eloquent room and slid on the shiny hard wood floor as the sound of the revolver yet echoed around the room and down the hall outside.

Doctor Adolf was startled, to say the least; while the others stood there in utter disbelief and bewilderment, wondering why.

Cardinal Bishop Francesco got weak in his legs and had to catch himself on the edge of the desk to keep from falling while he desperately struggled not to faint.

"Now that's what um talking bout!" Shouted General Amad, waving his arms in the air as he turned about in excitement. "House cleaning. You can't be scared to clean house."

"House cleaning? But why?" Doctor Adolf asked, trying desperately to hide his anger and disbelief, knowing full well that he could just as easily be next. "He was my brightest assistant. Why?"

"Nothing and no one is as good or better than I. You hear me? No one!" The President shouted smoothly, keeping his composure.

He bent down over the dead assistant, lying there with a large bullet hole in the front of his forehead, and with the back of his head blown off and laying several feet away across the room. Blood seeped out and gathered under his body, quickly clotting like clumps of jelly.

President Abu Nebuchezz stuck his little pinky finger into some of the dead man's blood and then slowly stuck his finger in his mouth as though he was tasting a delicately delicious meal. He held his finger in his mouth for a moment, with his eyes shut and his head tilted slightly towards the ceiling, as though relishing every taste of the fallen man's crimson blood.

"Nothing like the taste of warm blood," he said, as he slowly eased his finger out of his mouth. "My granddaddy use to say that nothing increases a man's life and vitality like rich warm blood after it has just been spilled. Even that heathen bible of theirs says that the life is in the blood. Y'all ought to try it"

He stood back up and wiped his finger on Eskandor's chest while he spoke to Doctor Adolf.

"So tell me how does it work, or shall I say, how do I work." Abu Nebuchezz said, as he motioned for some soldiers, that had rushed in after the shot, to remove the slain man's body. "Come.. come, show me; show me."

The President walked over to the adjacent bay window and sat easily on its ledge as he waited for a demonstration of the android's abilities.

Nervously, Doctor Adolf removed a black metal gadget from his pocket and pressed a little red button on top of it, and the android brang to life.

Cardinal Bishop, now sweating profusely, unknowingly stepped backwards a few steps, for he couldn't believe what he was seeing. It was an exact image of President Abu Nebuchezz. He knew what was happening and what the president was doing. It was prophecy fulfilling itself. Everything that the Bible had said would happen after the rapture, was happening right before his very eyes. He shivered all over in hidden fear, for he knew what was to come next. He knew that things were about to become worst, much, much worst.

He remembered his seminary training in eschatology on the android beast in the book of Revelation 13: 15-17: And he had power to give life unto the image of the beast, that the image of the beast should both speak and cause that as many as would not worship the image of the beast should be killed. 16. And he caused all, both small and great, rich and poor, free and bond, to receive a mark in their right hand, or in their foreheads. 17. And that no man might buy or sell, save he that had the mark, or the name of the beast, or the number of his name.

Yes, yes, the Bible was fulfilling its prophecy, but he knew that he was doomed to a life of eternal punishment because he had already received the mark of the antichrist-President Abu Nebuchezz. Cardinal Bishop Francesco dropped his head in the locks of his shoulders wreaking in hopeless despair.

The android looked sternly at the President, "How might I serve you Mr. Prsident?" The android asked with the expression of a real human man-President Nebuchezz utter twin.

"Well, what can it do?" General Amad asked.

"He is not an IT; he is a man- living computer that is wirelessly connected to the main computer in the basement of this building. He can do everything that you can do, but better. He can repair himself and all the computers in here, and he is connected to all computers around the world, and he is connected to every piece of military equipment that we have in our arsenal. He can launch missiles, even nuclear missiles that can destroy an entire nation or the whole world if you wanted him to. He doesn't need an extra code or another person to agree with him before launch. He is autonomous. He controls all the drones equipped with weapons; he can even control the satellites in space, and can locate anybody anywhere in an instant and give them a mark and a number from his location. He is forever learning and only you, Mr. President controls him. He is connected to your nervous system and your brain waves. Your thoughts are his thoughts.

"It can do all that?" General Amad asked, scratching his head in disbelief.

"Oh he can do much more than that," said Dr. Adolf, smiling with pride. "Much much more; I promise."

"What do you want to name him Mr. President? Only you will call him by the name that you give him. Everybody else will simply know him as you-President Abu Nebuchezz."

"I shall call him Me."

"Me?" Eskandor said, staring sternly at the android.

"Yes, Me, because he is me, and I am he. After today, when we part, you all want know who it is that you are talking to when we meet-Me or Me the other me. It is brilliant isn't it." He smiled broadly while he rubbed his hand through his long locks of hair. "I said that it is brilliant isn't it."

"Yes, yes Mr. President it is brilliant." They all chimed in. General Amad even clapping as he spoke.

"So Me, can you give us a demonstration," said The President to the android.

"Yes sir Mr. President. As you wish."

"You will no longer refer to me as president. You will refer to me as Me. That way, no one will know which of us is which when we in one another's presence. Do you understand me Me?

"Yes me; I understand you."

"Now give me a demonstration." Abu Nebuchezz ordered.

Suddenly the android snatched the little black box out of Doctor Adolf's hand and slammed it to the floor, and then stomped it with his feet, and grabbed Doctor Adolf by his neck and lifted him high into the air while squeezing, he broke his neck. He released Doctor Adolf, and his limb body fell hard to the floor.

They all, except President Abu Nebuchezz, gasped and stepped back, staring in utter horrified surprise.

"And?" The President asked smoothly to the android. "Why?"

"Nobody controls us, but us!" The android said, mimicking every movement and gesture that the president made. "We are one, and will destroy any and all that will get in our way of ruling the entire world."

"Can you make more like you, but don't look like us, or have the complete power that you have," asked the president.

"it is being done as we speak Me. They are being delivered all over the world in preparation for the upcoming world war against those rebels and folk of the church. All that will not join us, or receive our mark on their forehead or on their hand, will be destroyed.

"Time to go to war and separate the wheat from the tares. They'll worship me or die. I'll send them all to hell-if there be such a place." President Abu Nebuchezz said as he turned and glared out the big bay window. "Me, you remain here with me; we've got a few plans to set in motion before this day is done."

CHAPTER FOURTEEN

The war of Armageddon

The Seven Vials of God's wrath

Revelation 16

Revelation 16: 2: First vial: a noisome grievous sore upon the men which had the mark of the beast, and upon them that worshiped the beast.

Revelation 16: 3: Second vial: The sea became as the blood of a dead man, and everything died in the sea.

Revelation 16: 4: Third vial: Rivers and fountains became blood.

Revelation 16: 8: Fourth vial: Men scorched with great heat from the sun

Revelation 16: 10: Fifth vial: Men are filled with great pain and sores all over their bodies.

Revelation16: 12 Sixth vial: The Euphrates river dried up to make wake for the pagan kings to attack Israel for the battle of Armageddon.

Revelation 16: 17: Seventh vial: The earthquake shook the entire world that sank entire mountains and islands; Hail stones of ice weighing 130 pounds slammed to the earth.

Red dark grey ominous clouds hanged angrily in the never ending shaded blue lowering sky. The wind blew stiffly from the east carrying hints of sand, litter, and anything else that it could remove out of its place. It howled softly of impending forthcoming doom and suffering on the way.

Grumbling people stirred the solemn streets like zombies looking for a fresh grave to hide in. Their undiscernible voice saturated the angry day with burrows of hopelessness. Filled with pain and suffering, and opened puss filled wounds, they eased stiffly and aimlessly towards anywhere but where they were-hoping to run from the wrath that they knew was to come, but still their hard hearts refused them the humility to repent to the most high God who is always quick to issue out unwarranted mercy to all that would ask of him.

"Ok, Ok, where are we going? Where are we going Morrow." Snow asked, trying to keep up with Morrow galloping pace. "I don't remember nothing, then before I can gather myself, here come these big bad locust that killing everybody but us, and not to mention their leader, an "angel" Apollyon introducing himself and calling you an angel. Are you really an angel, or was that angel dude just shooting us some heavy smoke? I mean, what's going on, and how do I fit in the grand scheme of things?"

Snow spoke quickly between breaths as he tried to keep up with Morrow who was almost at a trot.

Suddenly, Snow stopped in his tracks and folded his arms, while he caught his breath.

"Just go on. Just go on to where ever it is that you are in such a hurry to go. I'll see you when I see you Morrow," said Snow between labored breaths.

Snow looked around to view just where he was. It looked like every other town that he had been through lately; tore up and filled with pain and suffering.

"Ok, Ok, you humans are so frail. Gosh, I wish I had my wings, but they are coming; I can feel them growing." Morrow spoke with mixed emotions as he walked back to Snow. "why you always have to know everything? Why can't you just be obedient and faithful for once in your puny life? Boy you had better be glad that you're no angel because you would have to walk everywhere."

"And why is that?" Snow eased out.

"Cause you would always lose your wings. Why you think I am walking. Snow, you got to learn how to do what you are told, when you are told, and how you are told without mumbling or asking any questions." Morrow said easing up to Snow. "Y'all had better be glad I am not God."

"Oh we are," said Snow. "There is no telling what you and that Apollyon fellow would have us doing."

"I was trying to reach Damascus before Armageddon start- The world war that will be fought right outside of Israel northern coastal plain the ancient city of Megiddo. I don't want to be there, just close enough to observe and maybe venture a little. You know, fight without being in the fight." Morrow said, still walking briskly.

"Huh."

"Yea, that's the war of wars discussed in the book of Ezekiel 38th chapter. Now that I think of it, Damascus might be a little too close."

"What war? What Ezekiel?" Snow stopped suddenly and grabbed Morrow by the arm. "I am not fixing to be involved in no war man. You hear me. Let them crazy folks have at each other. I don't have nothing to do with that stuff."

"You are in it whether you want to or not. It is an us against them kind of war. Saints against sinners; demons against angels. You get it now? And like it or not, you on one or the other side." Morrow spoke and gleaned straight down into Snow's very soul.

"What? What? What? All this is happening too fast." Snow grabbed his head as if trying to sturdy himself. "I ain't never seen that in the Bible."

"That is because you never read the bible. Look, look here at Ezekiel 38; lets read it for ourselves-huh."

Instantly an old Bible appeared in Morrows hands. He opened it to chapter 38, and there, in the middle of nowhere, they had a Bible study of Ezekiel 38. Morrow began to read.

"Behold it is come, and it is done, says the lord God; this is the day where of I have spoken.

And they that dwell in the cities of Israel shall go forth, and shall set on fire and burn the weapons, both the shields and the bucklers, the bows and the arrows. And the hand staves, and the spears, and they shall burn them with fire seven years.

So that they shall take no wood out of the field, neither cut down any out of the forests; for they shall burn the weapons with fire, and they shall spoil those that spoiled them, and rob those that robbed them, says the Lord God."

Morrow stopped reading and looked sternly over at Snow to see whether he was understanding the full gravity of the this situation of war that they were about to experience.

Snow gazed at Morrow with his mouth hanging open in amazement. "All snap, you mean that's about to go down here? Right now? Well, what are we going there for?"

"Cause, like it or not, we are a part of it. We are a part of the holy army of angels and men fighting demons and men."

Suddenly, Morrow kneeled to the grown with his head lowered in the locks of his shoulders. He moaned and groaned loudly as though he was in much pain.

Snow leaned forward to help him.

"No...No...No, stay back; stay back. Don't touch me!" Morrow shouted to Snow with his head still buried in his shoulders and hands clasping his head. His whole body began to glow a brilliant aluminous light that encapsulated his entire body. Snow could only see the light that now bathed his body, for Morrow was now completely consumed by the brilliant light.

His old reaction to danger eased upon him, and he reached around to his back to grabbed his pearl handled 9 millimeter, but he had forgotten that he does not carry a gun anymore; so whatever was happening to Morrow, he had to face it bare handed. He wondered whether the strange light was coming for him next.

The brilliant light lifted Morrow several feet from the ground and just floated there. It began slowly turning around and around. Snow still could not see Morrow.

He started to run, but couldn't. How could he leave Morrow who had saved him more times than he could count. No, he couldn't leave him; he refused to.

Suddenly, about twenty feet of feathered wings burst forth from amongst the light and glowed a titanium white. It eased slowly back to the ground while the glowing wings still stood regally.

After all of the aluminous light had gone, there stood Morrow with his head still hanging in the locks of his shoulders.

"Is…Is that you Morrow? Is it really you?" Snow asked nervously, still wondering what was happening to Morrow. He reflected back to when that angel over those horrible locust, had said that Morrow was an angel. He just couldn't believe that he had been in fellowship with a real angel. He just couldn't believe it, but there he was with wings and everything.

"Yes, it is I, Morrow, angel of the morning. I am back and better. Yes, I have learned as I lived amongst the humans as a human. I've learned how much strength is required to be human enveloped by such a weakened flesh. I have felt their pain and sorrow, and even their times of arrogance and pride. I have cried with them, fought alongside of them, and even many times against them. My hope in human kind is established. I guess that this was the Creator's original plan for me; for like Lucifer, I could not understand His love and protection for that creature He calls man. Every time He created one, they always fail, but He watched over them still. I have learned, and for that, I am better. I can serve the Creator better, and assist mankind better, particularly in this time of judgement tribulation."

Snow just stood there gazing with his mouth open, trying to fully take in what had just happened and what Morrow had just told him. He couldn't believe the sight of this new Morrow glowing with wings and all.

The old ragged clothes that Morrow had on, was now gone. His entire attire was white and illuminating.

"So…so, now what?" Snow stumbled to say.

"We shall assist from right here."

"Assist who? What? For what?" Snow asked, filled with a ton of questions.

"The battle of Armageddon is about to unfold. The battle that Ezekiel spoke of. " Morrow spoke, turning towards Jerusalem. "It is the coming world war to annihilate

Abraham's seed. Lucifer has been trying to do since the Creator's promise to him."

"What? A world war?"

"Yea, many shall attack Israel; only a few will stand with them. Russia, China, Ethiopia, Persia, Libya, Turkey, Iraq, Iran, Assyria, and many others shall fight together and forge an alliance against Abraham's children- just to name a few of the attackers. They will use all of their weapons, even nuclear weapons and chemical ones too, but they shall fail. For Abraham is God's beloved."

"You mean all of them are going to fly over to attack Israel? " Snow questioned.

"No, many will come by land; that's the reason why the Euphrates and Tigress rivers are dried up-to allow some to attack by land-especially Iraq, Iran, and Turkey."

"Well, why don't God just come and wipe them all out? I always thought that those were some crazy folk; they just want to fight for the sake of fighting. Look, every time that you turn on the T.V, or listen to the radio, you hear of them fighting or blowing up somebody. I know....I know, all of them aren't bad, so what do we do; just let them keep on killing us for pleasure."

"No, they want to destroy Israel, but we'll not allow it to happen, that's why all of my brothers are assemble here at the mountain of Armageddon. " Morrow said shifting his gaze upward to the sky as though looking at something or expecting something to appear.

His titanium wings eased to his side, displaying his broad shoulders and sculpture form. He lowered his head and slightly bent his knees, and in an instant, he was zooming upward in the sullen sky.

"Well, just leave me here, why don't you." Snow said, staring up at Morrow as he disappeared amidst the billowing clouds.

Snow looked off in the distance and saw something coming his way with a hail of dust behind it. He could tell that whatever it was, it was moving fast, very fast. He dashed behind a large boarder and peered around it as the ball of dust got closer and closer.

Although Snow couldn't clearly see it, it was V and Willie in the red mustang, now looking beige because of all the dust that had settled upon it.

The car pulled on to the side of the road-just about thirty feet from the boulder that Snow was hiding behind. He peered out easily and quietly around the rock to see just who it was, and what were they running from, though there was a lot for them to be running from now-a-days.

"Where are we, and why did you come down this road V?" Willie asked looking all around outside of the car to see what he could see. "Looks like we are in the middle of nowhere. Ain't nobody around us for miles. Boy, you sure got us in a hot mess this time. I mean, Lord have mercy."

"Willie, just shut up. I can't think with all that complaining you are doing. I got to get out and see where we are." She said.

"Good luck with that. I bet you google can't even find us out here-where ever this place is." Willie complained.

Snow eased out from behind the boulder and stared hard over at V and Willie-not believing what he was seeing.

"V." He whispered softly, not believing what he was seeing. "V!" He shouted out at them.

V and Willie was still arguing about where they were. They both turned to see who that it was calling her. She recognized Snow; a little bit thinner, but it was definitely Snow. She put her hands to her face while tears raced down her cheeks. She couldn't believe who she was seeing.

"Oh hell nawl!" Willie yelled out in disbelief. "Excuse me Lord." He said, looking up to the sky.

V ran and leaped up into Snow's arms. They hugged tightly and kissed as Snow swirled her around and around amidst labored tears of joy and relief.

Just then, several nuclear rockets raced across the sky, headed for Megiddo, the place of the beginning of the last world war-Armageddon. Moments later, a loud consuming blast thundered in the ears. They looked towards Megiddo as a mushroom cloud shot up in the sky towards the heavens.

"Oh God, that ain't what I think it is, is it? Oh Lord please let it go some place far out to sea or in the desert or some place." Willie screamed, holding his head as though it would drop off in a moment. "Why did we come all this way for this? I mean, come on now; to be blown away over a war that we don't have anything to do with."

"At least I got to spend my last moments with you." Snow moaned at V, still looking at the dark bright pinkish red mushroom cloud that had reached up to the heavens and started sending radioactive shockwaves, racing hundreds of miles an hour,

They all knew what was to come next....There was no escape; they were just too close to ground zero.

"Yes, If I must die, I'll die happily in the arms of the man I love." She laid her head upon his chest and closed her eyes, knowing full well what was on the way.

"We ought to run or something. Let's get in the car and out run that shock wave, or whatever it's call." Willie said, motioning for them to come on'

V and Snow didn't move, just kept on holding each other tightly.

"We choose how we go out-in faith and hope, or in desperate fear." Snow said, still gazing up at the mushroom cloud. "I choose hope. I shall rest today with my savior."

Willie, with his head dropped down, walked over and put his arms around both of them and held on tightly; time had run out.

The radiation raced across the sky at the speed of light, blasting away and vaporizing everything that was in its path. It reached Snow, V, and Willie, still embracing. They were consumed as they stood there. Their skin and flesh now gone; all that remained were three standing skeletons. The retraction of the blast, headed back to its core, swept the bones away as they turned to radioactive dust. In a moment, all three of them were gone along with hundreds of thousands of others that were in and around Armageddon.

THE WAR OF ARMAGEDDON HAD BEGUN!!!

Printed in the United States
by Baker & Taylor Publisher Services